Under the Mistletoe

Secret Heart Ink #4

༚

DEBORAH COOKE

Copyright © 2019 Deborah A. Cooke

All rights reserved.

ISBN-13: 978-1-989367-45-2

Books by Deborah Cooke

CONTEMPORARY ROMANCE

The Coxwells:
Third Time Lucky
Double Trouble
One More Time
All or Nothing
Christmas with the Coxwells

Flatiron Five:
Simply Irresistible
Addicted to Love
In the Midnight Hour
Some Guys Have All the Luck
Going to the Chapel
Bad Case of Loving You
Some Like it Hot (2020)

Secret Heart Ink
Snowbound
Spring Fever
One Hot Summer Night
Under the Mistletoe

PARANORMAL ROMANCE

The Dragonfire Novels
Kiss of Fire
Kiss of Fury
Kiss of Fate
Winter Kiss
Harmonia's Kiss
Whisper Kiss
Darkfire Kiss
Flashfire
Ember's Kiss
Kiss of Danger

Kiss of Darkness
Kiss of Destiny
Serpent's Kiss
Firestorm Forever
Here Be Dragons

The DragonFate Novels:
Maeve's Book of Beasts
Dragon's Kiss (2019)

The Dragons of Incendium:
Wyvern's Mate
Nero's Dream
Wyvern's Prince
Arista's Legacy
Wyvern's Warrior
Kraw's Secret
Wyvern's Outlaw
Celo's Quest
Wyvern's Angel
Nimue's Gift

The Prometheus Project
Fallen
Guardian
Rebel
Abyss

SHORT WORKS
An Elegy for Melusine
Coven of Mercy

☙

For information about Claire Delacroix historical romances, please visit:

HTTP://DELACROIX.NET

PROLOGUE

December 17—near Honey Hill, Maine

Liv was watching Spencer as he prepared dinner. It was snowing lightly but the forecast was for only a couple of inches of fresh snow. Spencer would have no problem getting to Wolfe Lodge in the morning and Liv planned to ride into town with him. She and Jane, the keeper of the bees, were making dried flower garlands for Lexi's wedding the following Sunday. They'd gathered and painted tree branches, and the entire process of decorating for the wedding was a lot more time-consuming than Liv had expected.

It was kind of fun, though.

And it made Liv think about her own future.

As had become their habit, she met Spencer in the kitchen of his cabin after he'd served dinner at the lodge and they had a late meal together. Although Spencer had been teaching her to cook, mostly on the weekends, during the week, he always had a plan. He said it was faster for him to cook and her to watch, and he always poured them each a glass of wine before he started to *mise en place*. As he worked that night, he told her about the deliveries for Lexi and Gabe's wedding reception, and again expressed his concern that the free-range turkeys might be too small to serve all the guests. Liv tried to reassure him, but knew already that he was a perfectionist about the meals he served.

Lexi and Gabe's wedding feast was one that Spencer wanted to get just right.

He was making chicken tonight, with a tomato herb sauce. He had fresh pasta from the woman who regularly delivered it to the lodge. The chicken had already been seasoned and browned and was sitting in a dish on the back of the stove. It smelled delicious.

Liv was amazed that she wasn't getting fat, just living with this man, but then, they did get a fair bit of aerobic exercise later each night. That made her smile as she sipped her wine and gathered her nerve.

It would have been a lot easier to ask if she hadn't already turned him down once.

"What's up?" Spencer asked, obviously noticing her smile.

Liv liked how observant he was. "I've been thinking," she said and his smile broadened. He was dicing onions really fast so she was glad he didn't look up. That long knife flashed and she knew it was sharp. He always diced the onions last even though he often cooked them first.

"Doing what you do best." The onions went into the skillet and began to sizzle.

"Best?" She echoed, wanting to tease him. "I think there are other things I do well enough for them to be contenders for first place."

She earned a very intent look for that, one that made her blush to her toes because she knew what he was thinking. "I won't argue with that," he murmured. He stirred the onions and added the garlic. "But you are the brains of the operation."

"I could argue that."

"You could, but you'd lose. You're brilliant, Olivia. I'm not."

It was so refreshing that he was at ease with his abilities, especially in comparison to hers. Liv had been with guys who had been threatened by her intellect. The special thing about Spencer was that he made her feel more human and her life more rounded. "Don't underestimate yourself. I couldn't run a restaurant."

Spencer scoffed. "Right back at you. You'd probably run a tighter inventory than I do."

"But you do other things that I can't, like cook."

"You're learning."

"I'll never be as good with food as you are."

That made him smile again. "Is it a problem that we have different strong suits?" The diced tomatoes went into the pan and he turned down the temperature, stirring and watching. She knew he was still listening to her, though.

This was the perfect opening. "No, it's really not," she said, her tone much more serious even though she hadn't planned it that way. She was just nervous and her words came out wrong.

Spencer noticed the difference immediately and pivoted to look at her, proof that she'd been right about him listening. "What's wrong?" he asked with concern. The sauce was simmering too hard, even Liv knew that, and she pointed to the pan behind him. He swore, lifted it off the burner and turned off the stove. He came to the other side of the island and leaned on it to look at her. "Tell me."

"There's nothing wrong..."

He lifted a brow.

"I just want to say something, to ask something, and it's important so I'm screwing it up." Liv reached for her wine but Spencer plucked the glass out of her hand, setting it aside.

"You can have it back when you're going to appreciate it," he said, then met her gaze again. His tone softened. "What's wrong, Olivia?"

"Nothing's wrong."

"You can tell me, you know. You have to know that by now." He leaned on the counter, wary. "We agreed that we could give it more time. I'm still good with that. I'm not trying to rush you."

"I know." Liv held up a hand when he would have argued with her. "Nothing's wrong, Spencer. Everything is right."

His eyes narrowed. "And that's a problem?"

"It's not what I expected."

"What did you expect?"

"That it would diminish. That we'd be less hot for each other and that our conversations would become less frequent and less interesting, and that we'd move into some kind of sustainable pattern of being together that was fine but not fabulous. I mean, the bar was pretty high. I thought it was too good between us and it couldn't last, that it couldn't stay so, so...hot." She took a breath. "So good. So potent."

Spencer didn't move. He didn't even blink.

"So when you asked me to marry you before, I thought it was too soon. I thought we were still in the bubble of the good stuff and that things would fizzle, even before we got to a wedding. That's why I said no, even though I wanted to say yes."

"But?"

"But I was wrong. It's still as good as it was in the beginning. In fact, that's not true—it's better." She looked at him and he nodded once in agreement. She flung out her hands. "It keeps getting better. It makes no sense. I keep missing you more during the day. I like making love to you more each time. I can't imagine not being with you. But nothing can expand infinitely. I keep thinking there has to be a limit and that it's going to be hell when we reach it."

"Aha," he said.

"Aha?"

"So, you feel vulnerable and you don't like that, so that's why you're dumping me." He frowned, exhaled and turned back to the stove. He moved the skillet and turned on the burner with a gesture that was more savage than it needed to be.

"I'm not dumping you," Liv said, astonished that he could make such a conclusion.

"But you're moving out," he concluded, his disappointment obvious. "I love you, Olivia, and I love being with you, but I'm not going to be an asshole about this. If you want to slow things down, or even if you want to end it, I love you enough to want you to be happy—with or without me." He added the herbs and stirred, then slid the browned chicken into the sauce. She waited until he put the lid on the pan, even though the tension between them was almost unbearable, and waited for him to face her again. His expression was impassive and he folded his arms across his chest, remaining by the stove as he surveyed her.

"I'm not moving out," Liv said firmly, wanting to get them out of danger. She eased off the stool and walked around the island, entering the sacred area of the kitchen that was his domain. "I don't even want to slow things down." She stopped right in front of him and tipped back her head to hold his gaze. She could smell his skin and feel the heat emanating from him, and the intensity in his gaze made her think of things they could do while dinner cooked.

"What then?" he said softly.

"I think I might be wrong, so I'd like to propose an experiment."

"An experiment, like this is some kind of science project or a clinical test? Olivia! This isn't a game! It's our lives!" He pushed his hand through his hair and would have turned away, but she put a hand on his arm and he froze.

"I hypothesize that there is something different about love, that it can, in fact, grow beyond all anticipated boundaries and continue to grow after that. It might, in fact, be limitless. I want to test the viability of an emotional bond over a lifetime—at least forty years but ideally more—under the additional constraint of a legal bond between the two parties."

He blinked. "What?"

Liv smiled. "Will you marry me, Spencer?"

He stared at her for a minute, then relief flickered into his gaze. "Just to prove that pair-bonding is sustainable and that love can continue to grow?"

"I think other people have proven that. I want to prove that *our* pair-bond is sustainable—and even that it's good for us." She swallowed. "I want to prove that love can become stronger over time, if the right pair-bond is chosen." She slid her hand up his arm, but he stepped away from her.

She'd been so sure of him.

Was he going to turn her down?

If so, it would be her own fault for declining his proposal the first time.

Panic flickered in her heart. What would she do without Spencer in her life? He was the constant one, the steady one, the predictable one. He was her rock and her anchor. What if he didn't want her anymore? The prospect made her dizzy.

He went to the bedroom and came back with something small in his hand. He smiled at her, looking a bit uncertain himself, then dropped to one knee before her. He opened his hand to reveal a black ring box. "I was going to ask you again at Christmas," he confessed and her heart sang with relief.

"But I want to be married before Christmas, so that would be too late."

"What's the sudden rush?"

"I want to be married first of the three of us, since I got the secret heart tattoo first. I want to be your wife at Lexi's wedding. I don't care if anyone else knows. I want to know that we're together for good."

"You're sure, then."

"I was sure before, just too chicken-shit to believe it."

"We can get the license tomorrow and be married by the end of the week by the Justice of the Peace, if that's what you want."

"That would be perfect! I don't care who's there, just us. Maybe my mom." Liv's throat was tight when Spencer slipped the ring onto her hand. It was a wide silver band with bees engraved on it. She turned it on her finger, examining it. "I love it! It's so beautiful! There's another one for you, right?"

He nodded and stood up, pulling her close. Liv couldn't imagine anywhere else she wanted to be. "This week?" he said, apparently still surprised.

"This week," she agreed, stretching to her toes to brush her mouth across his. "Then you'll be stuck with me forever."

"I can't imagine anything better," he murmured before he claimed her lips with a kiss. Liv wrapped her arms around his neck and kissed him back, happier than she'd ever been in her life. The little heart tattoo seemed to hum approval, almost like a bee in clover, and she smiled into his kiss, knowing she was exactly where she needed to be.

Forever.

CHAPTER ONE

Manhattan—December 22

It should be enough to help other people be happy.

Chynna had told herself so repeatedly, but there was a teeny part of her heart that didn't believe it. Was it selfish to want to be happy herself again? She'd had everything once and that was more than most people experienced. She should be glad to have been so lucky, not regretting her loss.

Again.

It was Christmas that made it harder. Being alone in the festive season was the worst, but making a bad connection just to fill a void would be stupid.

Tristan flew across the tattoo shop, making more noise about it than usual. He landed on the desk beside his trinket box, flapped his wings and fixed her with an expectant look.

"All right. I'm not alone. I have you," Chynna ceded.

He cawed and bobbed his head. She thought he'd rummage in his trinket box for something shiny, but he hopped over to the other end of the counter. It always made her smile to see him hop. The movement looked goofy, completely at odds with his usual dignity, and he spared her an indignant look as if he'd guessed her thoughts.

Then he plucked the envelope out of her pile of correspondence.

Chynna was startled. She didn't think Tristan had known it was there. It had come in the mail on a day when he'd been at her apartment, and she'd buried it beneath the bills a week before. She hadn't opened it or touched it, because she knew what it was.

Apparently, Tristan did, too.

He gripped the envelope in his beak and flew toward her, then landed on her shoulder. He dropped the envelope and she caught it instinctively. He bobbed his head, clearly pleased.

The envelope obviously contained an invitation.

It was a no-brainer that the invitation was to a wedding, given the pair of gold rings embossed on the envelope flap. The return address was Honey Hill, Maine, and she already knew that Lexi and Gabe were getting married at Christmas.

She'd already decided not to go, so there was no

need to open the envelope and feel that wave of envy that always embarrassed her.

She'd been lucky and she'd been loved. It was greedy to hope for more. She'd had her shot.

Tristan bobbed his head, as if to urge her to hurry and open the envelope.

"You probably aren't invited," she told him. "I don't need to open it to find that out."

He grunted.

"But I already know what it is. Lexi and Gabe are getting married. I'm not going."

There was a cry of protest from her companion. He leaned down and pecked at the corner of the envelope.

Chynna smiled in understanding. "Is that it? You're more concerned with the shiny paper than my social life?" She laughed lightly. "That figures. All right, I'll give you a piece." She tore open the flap and Tristan fluttered his wings in excitement at the gold foil lining inside. Chynna smiled and tore off the flap to give it to him. He seized it and flew across the shop to his trinket box, placing the piece of paper on top, then tucking it in with care. He admired it, adjusted it, then came back for another.

"You are greedy," she accused him, then pulled out the invitation just so she could rip the envelope apart for him. The little card to be used for her response fell to the floor along with its envelope.

He made a sound that she thought of as a quorl. It was a bird call but it sounded like a question to her.

"I told you. Lexi and Gabe." She read the invitation to him. "*Cordially invite your presence for their exchange of their vows December 23rd at Wolfe Lodge in Honey Hill, Maine.* That's nice. It'll be pretty, I'm sure."

Tristan made another question sound.

"Of course, I'm not going. You know I don't go to weddings. And I don't go anywhere at Christmas. I'll send them a nice card and my good wishes." She sighed. "And we'll have a special treat, just for us. I'll get you a chicken liver."

Tristan protested that she was taking too long, pecking at the envelope again. Chynna tore the foil-lined envelope into pieces along the folds, amused that the raven was almost jumping with anticipation. She gave him one piece at a time, watching him place each one in his trinket box. When he had them all, he remained perched on the side of it, rearranging his treasures with evident satisfaction.

If only everyone could be happy with just a piece of gold foil.

If only she could be.

Chynna sighed just as a man cleared his throat at the door to the shop. She made herself smile then turned to find Theo, one of the partners of the Flatiron Five fitness club, standing there. He was dressed to the nines in a beautifully cut charcoal suit with a red tie. Chynna preferred leather jackets to suits on men, but an elegant man like Theo could certainly make her think about changing her mind. He was a tall, trim black man and had a British accent. He was often in London but she thought he might have been from there originally. She didn't know much about him, but he was always charming.

He gestured with several envelopes and smiled. "Merry Christmas," he said. "Some of your mail came to the front desk. They look like bills, unfortunately."

"I could have just picked them up." Chynna took the envelopes and sifted through them. He was right. They were bills. She set them on the desk with her other correspondence.

"It's no problem. Gives me a chance to peek in."

She turned to find Theo surveying the tattoo shop, his curiosity obvious. "Damon designed the space," she said. "We had a talk about colors and light, and then he came up with this."

"Do you like it?"

"I love it. He's a very talented designer."

"So he is." Theo crossed the room to look down at her favorite tattoo gun as if it was an artifact from another planet. His caution amused her. "And you do a lot of tattoos here?"

"Yes, it's a great location for business."

"But you had another shop before, right?"

"I did. Imagination Ink. It's in Chinatown. It was time I passed it on."

"I don't understand."

"I did. Imagination Ink. It's in Chinatown. I sold it to Rox, who was working for me. She does the best dragon tattoos, by the way, if you ever need one."

He reached out to tentatively touch the tattoo gun, his finger hovering just above it. "Does it hurt?"

Chynna shrugged. "Everyone is different and every location is different. Arms aren't bad for most people. Hands can be tougher."

"So the short answer is yes."

"At the very least it burns a bit, but only for a while."

"You're not going to say 'no pain no gain'?"

Chynna smiled. "That's more of a slogan for your business than mine."

His eyes twinkled. "Then what would a slogan for your business be?"

Chynna looked around, thinking. "'Art hurts.'"

Theo's smile flashed. "I like it."

"I'll guess you don't have any tattoos."

"No." Theo spoke firmly.

"Blank canvas," she teased as he laughed.

"All original equipment," he replied easily.

"Thanks for bringing the mail."

Tristan croaked and bobbed his head. At first Chynna thought he was agreeing with her, but then he seized the invitation and flew toward Theo. In the last minute, he turned, dropped the invitation and landed on Chynna's shoulder. It was a smooth move and Chynna knew he'd intended to have the invitation fall at Theo's feet, practically on the toe of his beautifully polished leather shoe.

Theo bent down to pick it up, then smiled. "Is this a match from one of your secret heart tattoos?"

"It is." Tristan, quite helpfully, knocked the RSVP card to the floor from the desk.

This time, Chynna hurried to pick it up, but Theo had seen it and obviously guessed what its presence meant.

"Aren't you going?" He sounded surprised.

"No, I'm too busy this time of year," Chynna said, feeling herself blush. "I'll send them my good wishes."

Theo pointedly looked around the empty shop. "I don't see a line."

"Well, it can get crowded," Chynna said, knowing she sounded defensive.

She was.

"Why don't you want to go?" Theo asked gently. "You helped them find happiness. That's a party you should attend."

"Oh, I think it's too late to respond that I'm coming," she said quickly.

Theo glanced down at the invite, then spoke slowly. "There's an email address for replying. You could tell them now."

"I don't have a way to get to Maine."

"Take the train. Rent a car. It's not far."

Chynna sighed and fixed him with a look. He grinned at her, no doubt guessing that she was trying to avoid the festivities.

"Don't like weddings?" he asked.

"Don't do well at Christmas."

"All the more reason to go." He squared his shoulders and sobered a little. "I find that in challenging moments, it's better *not* to be alone."

"You have challenging moments?"

"Everyone does, Chynna." Theo averted his gaze, keeping his secrets. "And a lot of people have them over the holidays." He turned to smile at her again. "Be kind to yourself. This sounds like fun. There must be someone you can call to help you get there. Or the bride and groom might find a solution."

It sounded like advice Chynna would give someone else, but she still felt resistant to it. "I could call Reyna to meet me in Portland," she said slowly. "But I can't take Tristan on the train." Tristan croaked and bounced a little. "And I don't know anyone who would take him."

Theo smiled and stretched out a finger. "I can take him for a few days if you tell me what he eats." Tristan flew to Theo's finger before Chynna could decline and rubbed his beak on Theo's thumb. The two eyed each other like a pair of co-conspirators. Given that Tristan was usually slow to warm up to new friends, especially men, Chynna was a little startled by his obvious approval of Theo. "He wouldn't even have to leave the building."

"I don't have anything to wear," Chynna said and Theo laughed.

"If you brought the happy couple together, all they'll care about is that you're there to share their joy."

Chynna sighed and played her last card. "If I go, I'll have to go now to get there in time, so I won't be able to give away my secret heart tattoo at the club tonight. It's bad luck to stop something like this once you've started."

"That's your last excuse?" Theo teased.

"Yes."

"And if that were solved, you'd go?"

Chynna took a deep breath. "Yes," she agreed, pretty sure she wasn't risking much.

"Then give the tattoo to me," Theo said.

She was astonished, which only amused him. "Mar your blank canvas?"

"Well, it's a good cause. And it's just a little heart." He lifted his hand and Tristan flew back to his trinket box. Theo shed his suit jacket, folded it and laid it over a chair. He unfastened his cuffs and loosened his tie, then smiled at her as he removed his dress shirt. "Maybe it's a day for both of us to say yes when we're inclined to say no." He was wearing a white T-shirt under his dress shirt and it was skin-tight, showing every sculpted muscle to advantage.

Chynna was impressed and couldn't hide it. "Why haven't you been on one of the billboards for the club?"

"Cassie just hasn't gotten to me yet. Now that I'm stateside again, I fully expect her to spring a new marketing plan on me. Where do you want to put it?"

"You have to live with it, so you tell me." She made a stencil of the heart so he could approve the location before she tattooed it.

"Bicep."

"Good choice." She glanced up to find him watching her. "Pain-wise. You'll barely feel it there."

Theo nodded. "Right arm or left?"

"They're both perfect. It's up to you."

Theo touched his left bicep with his right index finger. "There."

"There," Chynna agreed. She applied the stencil in the location he'd chosen, then told him to look at it in the mirror. She watched, hoping for her favorite moment, not certain it would happen with Theo.

It did. He smiled, the curve spreading slowly over his lips, then lighting his dark eyes. "I like that," he said, turning to her, apparently surprised.

Chynna smiled back. "Good. Let's make it permanent." She patted the bench then tugged on her latex gloves. She loaded the gun with ink and set to work.

She was going to a wedding, and despite her earlier misgivings, she was starting to get excited about the trip.

She was giving Theo instructions on caring for the tattoo when Tristan hopped across the shop. He tugged out his deck of tarot cards so that they spilled all over the floor, then croaked at the mess.

"Tristan!" Chynna said, but the bird was pulling one card free. He hopped toward her and laid it at her feet, showing smug satisfaction in his choice.

"So, he does choose tarot cards," Theo said as he buttoned his shirt. "I'd heard that."

"Yes, he does."

"What does that card mean?"

"*The Lovers*," Chynna said. "Wild sex ahead." She met Theo's gaze, only to find him chuckling. "Looks like you'll be having quite the holiday this year. Is that why you decided to stay in Manhattan?"

"Not me," Theo said. "He gave *you* the card, Chynna."

Chynna blinked, because Theo was right.

"Don't melt all the snow in Maine," Theo teased and Chynna blushed. "Now tell me how to take care of Tristan, and you can get on your way."

Trevor was at loose ends.

He was working temporarily at Wolfe Lodge, but didn't know where he was going next. The plan had been to *stay* at the lodge and he'd been looking forward to it.

He'd arrived to take Gabe's place when Gabe left Maine, and the timing had been great. Trevor had been between restaurants, having sold one and still seeking a new opportunity. He'd been glad to come to Honey Hill and he loved what Spencer and Gabe had done with Wolfe Lodge. There was a lot of opportunity for growth and he'd just started making plans for the new year when Gabe had returned.

As glad as Trevor was that Gabe and Lexi were getting married, he was a little out of sorts that what had looked like a dream job had dissolved in his hands. He was staying for the near future, filling the gaps while Gabe and Lexi arranged their wedding, then he'd manage things while the happy couple took their honeymoon.

Filling in temporarily wasn't the same as making the place his own. Gabe had invited him to stay on as an assistant, but Trevor knew it was better for both of them if he moved on. He liked to be completely invested in anything he did. Half-measures weren't his style and neither was reporting to anyone else. He was all-in or all-out, in charge or not involved. Worse, he felt the need for a big new challenge, like the one he could see around him at Wolfe Lodge.

Even the fact that he wasn't leaving just yet was weird. Trevor didn't wait around for much of anything. But he and Gabe went way back and he wanted to help Gabe. He supposed it wasn't all bad to have a job while he took the time to find the right opportunity.

When had he last had just a job? Trevor couldn't remember if that had ever been the case. His work had always been closer to an obsession.

He'd built many restaurants to success then sold them. That didn't feel like a challenge anymore. The lodge had interested him because it was more than a restaurant, more than a bar. As a resort, it offered many more challenges and opportunities. It felt like it would take a while to get it established and that there would be challenges to conquer on the way.

It felt like it might be a place he could stay. Even though the idea of setting down roots made him twitchy, Trevor wasn't one to be stopped by his own doubts. He'd recognized that he had a concern, and he was going to eliminate it.

Wolfe Lodge would have been the perfect location for that. He knew that Gabe was feeling much the same way and could understand his colleague all too well. Trevor wasn't sure where to find a similar opportunity. At the very least, he'd need to find a resort that was performing beneath its possibilities, then add a great chef and his own magic.

At the most, he'd have to start from the ground up, buying land and building a resort. That seemed to Trevor to be a bit too big of a challenge to assume on his own. It would be an awesome triumph, if it succeeded, but he was at the point in his life that he wanted to share his success with someone else.

He wanted to be all-in on a different kind of endeavor, like Lexi and Gabe, like Spencer and Liv.

That was even more elusive than a lodge in need of his abilities.

To find both, a life challenge and a life partner, seemed against the odds.

Trevor was lonely. He'd finally admitted it to himself, and it shocked him. He was thirty-eight, affluent, without ties of any kind. He had a huge circle of friends but always went home alone. He had a hundred people he could call to meet for lunch or a drink, maybe more, but no one he'd call an intimate friend. For a long time, solitude had been ideal, as he threw himself into new projects with such abandon that he didn't even have time to sleep, let alone nurture a relationship. He liked to be able to move whenever he sold out and found a new opportunity. More than one woman had walked away from him over his driven life. Often, it had taken him days to notice.

Something had changed with the sale of his last restaurant. His parents had passed away, his brother was married with toddlers, and there'd been no one close to share his celebration. That wasn't new, but his awareness of it was.

Trevor noticed the hole in his life, and as was typical of him, resolved to fill it ASAP. He wanted a relationship that could be the rock on which he built his future. He felt that even if he accepted the challenge of establishing a successful resort, it would be empty without someone to share the joy. He wanted to do things differently, but it had been a while since he had met a woman who caught his eye, never mind held his interest.

That all changed when *she* walked into the party in Honey Hill.

Damn.

He stopped cold and stared.

She was urban. Sleek. Gorgeous. Trevor felt that lightning bolt of recognition and knew she was the one.

Too bad she didn't even seem to have noticed him.

He could fix that.

It was after nine, three days before Christmas, and the day before Gabe and Lexi's wedding. The party at their house in Honey Hill was just getting started. The fairy lights strung all over the house were sparkling. The wine was flowing—and so was the champagne—and the kitchen was filled with the smell of hors d'oeuvres coming out of the oven. Spencer was holding court there, laughing with friends as he served up his creations. People had come from Portland, Bangor, and even Boston for the party and the noise level was already high. Lexi had invited her new neighbors, and Reyna, the former owner of the house, was admiring the changes already made to it.

The world didn't stop when the new arrival stepped into the kitchen, but Trevor's world lurched to a halt. Like many of the guests who had come for the wedding from out of town, she'd dressed up for the party. She wore a sleeveless sheath of glittering black sequins that hugged her slender figure. She wore short black boots with it, witchy little boots with spike heels and pointed toes. Her hair was short and so fair that it was either white-blond or dyed silver. Her long bangs had magenta tips. She carried a black brocade coat that she'd already removed in the front room and a clutch purse. Her lipstick matched the tips of her hair and her eyes were lined with dark eyeliner that made her look both delicate and exotic.

Her most striking adornment, though, was her

Under the Mistletoe

ink. She had tattoos covering both arms—full sleeves—of roses spilling from her shoulders to her wrists. They were so detailed that Trevor halfway thought he could smell their perfume from across the room.

She waited at the threshold of the kitchen, just looking, and Trevor seized the moment. He went to greet her.

"Hi," he said with a smile and she smiled back. "Can I hang up your coat for you?"

"I didn't realize the party would be catered."

"It's not, really." He indicated Spencer. "We just can't forget our day jobs."

She laughed and he liked how low her voice was. Sultry. Mesmerizing. "You don't look like a coat check girl."

Trevor grinned and offered his hand. "Trevor Graham, temporary manager of Wolfe Lodge and lifelong survivor of the hospitality biz."

"Wolfe Lodge? I'm staying there."

"Pretty much everyone is. Smart of Gabe to book the wedding for a week that's usually slow, but then, he's an excellent resort manager."

"You've known him a long time?" Chynna surrendered her coat and Trevor moved toward the rack. He kept talking to her, hoping she'd follow.

She did.

"Close to twenty years. Been competitors more than once."

She smiled. "Who won?"

"One here, one there. I think it shakes out pretty

evenly, actually."

She laughed lightly and offered her hand. "I'm Chynna," she said and he had the urge to kiss her hand. She looked so regal and feminine, yet hardly in silk and pearls. He thought her balance of elegance and edge was exactly perfect.

He smiled as he shook her hand and looked into her eyes. She flushed just a little and his own smile broadened. They were off to a good start.

"Chynna!" Lexi cried then and came to hug the new arrival. "Look at what you've done." She held up her left hand, showing her engagement ring.

"Me?" Chynna protested, her eyes sparkling. "I haven't done anything."

"You pushed me toward the possibilities," Lexi argued. "You encouraged me to take a chance." She sighed and smiled, her happiness obvious. "You might end up with kids named after you."

"Oh, I think I can survive that."

"Godchildren," Lexi threatened. "Who will want to come to visit when they're teenagers and beg for tattoos from you."

Chynna laughed.

"You're a tattoo artist?" Trevor asked and she nodded.

"*The* tattoo artist," Lexi said, beckoning to Reyna. "Come on over here and let Trevor admire Chynna's work."

"My human canvas," Chynna said with a smile. Reyna was wearing a halter dress in brilliant red, with a swing skirt, one that reminded Trevor of

Marilyn Monroe standing over a grate. She had a strong sense of style, which he'd often admired. He thought of her as the rockabilly queen of Honey Hill.

"Be awed, people." Reyna turned in place, showing off the ink that covered her arms and back. Her companion, Kade, watched with a smile. He was a cop in Portland and looked like one to Trevor, his calm assessing gaze matched with quiet confidence. They were an attractive couple, one conservative and one outrageous, but the way their gazes locked was an eloquent sign of the powerful feelings between them.

Liv joined the group then, also greeting Chynna with a hug and kiss. She was an academic, very cute, and living with Spencer. Spencer and Gabe were introduced to Chynna and Trevor thought he might get pushed out of the little group. She smiled at him, though, and he held his ground.

She was worth the wait.

"But where's Tristan?" Lexi asked and Trevor feared that Chynna had a partner.

"They don't let birds on the train," she said. "And even if they did, Tristan would be trying to collect shiny souvenirs. A friend is raven-sitting for me."

She had a pet raven.

Trevor was officially intrigued.

The party ebbed and flowed as the best ones do, and Chynna moved closer to the island loaded with hors d'oeuvres. More guests arrived and Lexi went to greet them, Reyna turning to Kade with a murmured joke.

"Would you like a drink?" Trevor asked Chynna and her eyes sparkled.

"That hospitality business gets in your blood."

He laughed. "It does."

She moved closer to him and he could smell her perfume. She wore a fine chain around her neck and it hung as if there was a weight on it. Whether it was a pendant or other souvenir, it was hidden beneath the neckline of her dress. He was curious.

"I don't know anything about wine," she confessed.

"You're in luck: I do."

"I thought you might."

"What are your preferences? Red? White? Sweet? Dry?"

She surveyed the platters and indicated one. "I'd like to try one of those scallops, so I'd like a wine that will play nicely with them."

"Done." Trevor said and poured two glasses of champagne. Her eyes widened in surprise. "They're wrapped in bacon, and the best match for salt and fat is champagne."

"Really?"

"Really. Try it with take-out Chinese food sometime."

She tried to keep from laughing and failed. "Pizza?"

He made an okay sign with his hand. "Ideal match, especially if there's sausage or pepperoni on it. Try it if you don't believe me."

"I will."

He gave her a glass and their fingertips brushed in the transaction. He lifted his glass to her, inviting her to toast with him. "Welcome to Honey Hill."

"Thank you, Trevor." Their gazes clung as they sipped in unison and Trevor knew he wasn't the only one interested.

She'd come for the wedding, so she'd be gone in two or three days. He didn't have a lot of time to waste.

He passed her the platter of scallops and a small plate. "How do you know Lexi?"

Chynna had been hungry by the time she'd arrived at the lodge, and had hoped there'd be food at the party in town to welcome the out-of-town guests. She'd barely stepped in the door when she discovered that she had an appetite for more than food.

One look at Trevor, and Chynna wanted to be naked with him. It was an uncommon reaction for her and a primal one, but that didn't make it any less powerful. Chynna's own tiny heart tattoo, the original of the secret heart tattoos, given to her by the first Tristan in her life, seemed to pulse.

As if his ghost approved.

The simple truth was that she was due for a fling. Past due, even. She was due for a reminder that Tristan had died, not her. It was time to move on, just a little. She'd never forget him and she'd never replace him, but she could have a little fun.

Tristan would have encouraged it.

That man had been all about fun and savoring the moment.

His attitude had been a big part of the reason she'd fallen in love with him.

Chynna reminded herself that she was on vacation, in a way, at this wonderful lodge. She'd be home again in three days, in time to have Christmas at home, and whatever happened here would be left behind.

Wolfe Lodge offered the perfect opportunity for a hook-up.

The raven she'd named after her beloved partner had drawn that tarot card, after all, as if the bird had been channeling Tristan and advising her to do just that.

The Lovers.

Trevor was about her age with dark hair and dark eyes, tall and trim. She guessed that he worked out, just by the way he moved. There was something graceful and almost predatory about him, as if he was a puma in the middle of the night. His dark eyes seemed to be filled with mysteries, the kind of secrets a shape shifter might have. He was protective of her, too, his manner making her think about being claimed by him. She liked the low rumble of his voice, the thread of humor she heard in it, and the flash of his smile made her heart skip.

She could be a destined mate for a night.

Maybe two.

Ha. Then she'd be back in New York, her urges satisfied—because she had no doubt that he would satisfy her—and the interlude at an end.

She liked how he came back to her at regular intervals, making sure she had a drink or an appetizer, or had met the person nearby. He wasn't overbearing but was obviously interested. His attention made her feel feminine and sexy.

How long had it been?

Chynna decided it wouldn't be one night longer. She had a glorious room, with a king sized bed and a massive bathroom, and on this night, she didn't want to sleep alone.

In fact, she didn't want to sleep at all.

Trevor was refilling her glass of champagne when she saw the tail end of a tattoo at the edge of his shirt cuff. It was on the back of his wrist, peeking out from beneath his watch.

"You have a tattoo!"

"Don't look so surprised."

"I didn't think you were the type."

His smile warmed her to her toes. "Come on, Chynna. In your business, you must see people of all types."

"It's true, and I know better than to judge a man by the cut of his suit. I apologize." She let her gaze sweep over that suit, ensuring her appreciation of him showed.

Trevor's grin widened and he leaned closer. The party was getting loud and she knew he wanted to make sure she heard him, but she liked having his heat close. His voice was almost a murmur, deep enough to make her shiver. His lips almost touched her cheek and she felt hot all the way to her toes. "I've been admiring yours. Those roses look so real."

Chynna smiled but didn't move away. "I know. They're wonderful. A very talented friend did them for me."

He dropped a finger to her bare shoulder and traced the outline of one flower. Chynna's mouth went dry. His touch was gentle, his fingertip warm, and he watched his hand, as if fascinated. She watched it, too. "There are a lot of good tattoo artists in New York," he said in a low rumble. "That's where I had mine done."

"Can I see it?"

Trevor pretended to be surprised. "Here and now?"

Chynna laughed. "Call it a professional interest."

"Here I was hoping you just wanted me naked," he said ruefully, his tone teasing. His dark eyes sparkled and Chynna placed her hand on his chest.

"Where does it say that I don't?" she whispered and his eyes lit.

"Show me yours and I'll show you mine," he offered.

Chynna laughed lightly, sure they'd do just that. She didn't want to surrender too quickly though because she was enjoying their conversation.

Trevor didn't back away but traced the outline of another rose. Chynna took that as a sign that he was content to let the heat build a little more between them, too. "And where do you do tattoos?"

"I'm one of those artists in New York."

"Clearly, one of the talented ones. Reyna's tattoos are terrific."

"Thank you. I used to own a shop called Imagination Ink, but I sold out to my partners. Now I have a smaller shop uptown in a fitness club. Flatiron Five. Maybe you've heard of it."

Trevor shrugged, then his brows drew together. "Wait a minute. Are you the one who gives the secret heart tattoos? Spencer's girlfriend, Liv, has one, Reyna has one and Lexi has one."

"Yes, that's me. The three of them came to the opening of my newer shop in March, and Liv got the first tattoo."

"Are they really magic?"

"I think so."

He met her gaze steadily. "They say the tattoos brought them true love."

Chynna couldn't tell whether he believed that or not. "That's what they're supposed to do." She shrugged. "That's why I was invited to the wedding."

"Maybe I should get one from you."

"You haven't found true love yet?" Chynna asked, then wondered if she'd asked too much.

Trevor wasn't insulted, though. "No. I was never much worried about it until lately."

"I can't believe you don't have any interest in women."

His smile turned wicked. "Let's just say I'm lucky at cards," he said and they laughed together. He indicated her glass. "Another?"

"Last call," Chynna agreed.

"I hope you're not going to abandon me here," he said, an invitation in his eyes.

Chynna liked that he left the choice to her. "I was hoping you weren't going to send me back to the lodge alone." She wrinkled her nose. "Such a cold winter night."

Their gazes locked and held. It was clear how much her words pleased him.

"We'll have to think of some way to stay warm."

"We will." Chynna couldn't take a full breath when he looked at her with such intensity. She had the feeling that he would be a leisurely lover, one who lingered and savored, and just the idea made her anxious to start.

"One more, to toast the happy couple," he suggested and she nodded agreement.

Trevor worked his way back to the island in the middle of the kitchen, because somehow they'd ended up several feet away. Chynna watched him go, her anticipation rising as she watched him joke with one person and another. He was charming, but he moved steadily toward his goal. Purposeful. She liked that. He had to get another bottle from the fridge and opened it, then filled the glasses with easy grace. He winked at her from across the room and her heart skipped as she watched him approach.

It had been so long since she'd seduced a man.

But then, she'd be back in New York soon. If she got it wrong, there was little chance of seeing Trevor again.

In fact, that made this an ideal opportunity to let loose.

CHAPTER TWO

It was so easy.

Like being together was meant to be.

Trevor drove Chynna back to the lodge and they rode in silence, but not an awkward one. They both knew where they were going and why. Unless he was a lot less perceptive than he thought he was, they were both excited about it, too.

He no sooner had the thought than Chynna cast him a wicked little smile. Her eyes were sparkling and she surveyed him, her smile turning devilish.

Oh yeah. They were definitely on the same proverbial page.

He parked in his usual spot and went around to get her door.

"There are so many stars," she said, tipping back her head to look. "In the city, I forget."

"In the city, there are brighter lights to look at,"

Under the Mistletoe

he said, then stole a kiss. She leaned against him, slipping her hands beneath his leather jacket and spreading them flat across his chest to explore him. Her hands eased around his back then her arms tightened around him, her breasts pressing against his chest. He echoed her movement, drawing her closer. She was soft and warm, and opening her coat released a waft of musky perfume.

He caught a whiff of her own scent, too, and that was all the encouragement he needed to kiss her more deeply. She opened her mouth to him, welcoming his touch with an abandon that stole his breath away.

He broke their kiss before they ended up doing it in the parking lot. She was flushed and a little out of breath, and her eyes were sparkling. Trevor guided her to the door. "Your place or mine?" he asked in the lobby and she laughed at him. The kid on the desk gave a wave and ducked into the office to answer a ringing phone.

"You're staying here, too?"

"It's the best place in town, if I say so myself."

"Whose room is bigger?"

"Mine, but yours is fancier."

"Yours," she said, slipping her hand into his. "I'm ready to see the sights."

"Honey Hill doesn't have many sights. There's the lake, and the stars..."

"And your tattoo," she said with resolve. "I want to see it all."

Trevor grinned and captured her hand, leading

the way. "You do just want me naked."

"Do you have a problem with that?"

"Not if you're going to get naked, too."

"Of course!" She bumped shoulders with him companionably as they walked down the corridor to his room. The contact was casual, as if they were buddies, but Trevor's reaction was a lot hotter than he'd feel with a friend. She was less mysterious than she had been and he wondered if she was changing her mind.

Or nervous.

But why?

He opened the door to his room and flicked the switch. The pair of table lamps were connected to it, and their light was soft. The main room looked welcoming, at least to his eyes. It was furnished by the lodge and cleaned by the housekeeping staff, but was his current home.

"A suite!" Chynna exclaimed, peeking into the bedroom.

"Just a small one. Don't miss my fabulous view of the parking lot." He always kept the drapes closed but Chynna went and peeked through the gap.

"Nice. I suppose the view of the lake is what guests want."

"Absolutely. How's your view?"

"It was dark when I got here so I'm not sure." She closed the drapes before surveying it again. "It looks more like an apartment than a hotel room."

She'd noticed the pictures and other personal

effects, then.

"I'm working at the lodge for a bit, so am living here, too. Would you like a drink?"

She shook her head. "Why don't you get an apartment? You'd have more privacy and a kitchen, too."

"With Spencer in the kitchen here at the lodge, all I need is a coffee pot. I'm not much of a cook. Are you?"

She averted her gaze and he sensed sadness in her. "I like to cook, but live on my own. I don't usually bother."

"You can cook for me," he offered, hoping to make her smile.

She did, then gestured to the coffee pot. "You don't have a kitchen."

Trevor laughed. "We can sneak downstairs in the middle of the night if you feel the urge."

"That's not the urge I'm feeling right now," Chynna said, looking sultry again. She took off her coat and Trevor took it from her to hang it up. By the time he turned back, she was unfastening the zipper in the back of her sequined dress and had kicked off her boots.

Maybe this was going to be quick.

He hoped not, but it was all good.

She dropped her dress over her shoulders and it fell to her waist. Her lingerie was more practical than fancy, which might mean she hadn't intended to go home with anyone. It might mean that she just didn't like lingerie. Trevor was one who cared more about what was inside it, but he chose to believe that she'd come home with him because there was magic between them.

Even though the magic seemed to have been dismissed in the parking lot.

He could see that there was a ring on that chain around her neck, a woman's ring. Why was it there? Didn't it fit anymore? Or was it a souvenir of a broken heart? Trevor wanted to know but knew better than to ask.

"Nice work," he said, studying her tattoos. The roses covered her arms in full sleeves, then continued across her shoulders, as if they sprouted from there. She didn't have a back piece, so maybe they came out of the void. Trevor realized that there was a hint of a trellis behind the roses, as well as little fairies hidden beneath the rose petals. He smiled at the whimsy of them, then noticed a spider, then another. There was a red heart in the hollow of her throat, almost like a medallion. He would have looked more but she tugged at his cuff with impatience.

"Let me see."

"Why roses?"

"Because they're about love, of course."

"And the fairies?"

"Because magic is everywhere, even when we forget to look for it." She'd answered these questions before, he could see.

"You're going to be disappointed," he said. "I only have one tattoo."

"I hope that means it's a good one."

"I think so. I thought about it for a long time. I think it's perfect." He removed his shirt, fully expecting to hear a gasp of surprise. She didn't make a sound, but then, Chynna was more accustomed to large tattoos than a lot of people. He turned around, expecting her to be studying the tattoo with professional interest.

Instead, she looked shocked. She was pale and her eyes were wide, her mouth open slightly in her astonishment.

But she was a tattoo artist, and millions of people had swimming koi tattoos. It was a classic. Trevor frowned. "I didn't think it would shock you. It's a pair of koi. Lots of people have them."

Chynna stretched out a hand and he saw that she was shaking. "When did you have this done?" she whispered.

"About twelve years ago. In New York. Really talented artist."

She swallowed, taking a step closer, her gaze roving over the tattoo. "Oh yes," she said, her voice a husky whisper.

Trevor was surprised that she was so emotional, then he had an idea. *She* was a tattoo artist from New York, after all. "Do you know Tristan?"

"Did," Chynna corrected, then met his gaze. "He's dead."

It was Trevor's turn to be shocked then. "You're kidding. I had no idea."

"Cancer. It was fast for him, at least." She

swallowed and Trevor realized she'd not just known Tristan: she'd been close to him. He watched her for a minute and saw how she struggled with her emotional reaction.

No, she'd loved that guy.

She still did.

He knew whose ring that was.

"Fuck cancer," he said quietly, feeling cheated on a number of fronts.

She shook her head, losing a single tear. It fell like a diamond to the carpet. "I'd rather not get that close." Her voice was husky, though she tried to smile.

"I'm sorry. I'm really sorry." Trevor didn't know what else to say. He figured everything had gone wrong then and she'd pull up her dress, make an excuse and leave. He really didn't want her to go, especially not when she was upset, but he wasn't sure what to say.

Everything he'd said since taking off his shirt had worked so brilliantly, after all.

"Don't be." Chynna reached out to touch his arm. She ran her fingertips from his shoulder to his wrist and he realized she was caressing the tattoo, not him. She took a deep shaky breath as if to steel herself.

With her fingertips, she followed the outline of the koi that was swimming down from his shoulder, then the one that swam up from his wrist. Her touch slid around waves and the lotus blossoms, her gaze fixed on the ink. Her touch made Trevor

Under the Mistletoe

shiver, and when she flattened her hand to make more contact and slid it back up again, he felt a surge of heat.

And desire.

He caught his breath and clenched his fists, not wanting to push her in this moment. The last thing he wanted to do was be a dick and intrude on her memories with his own desire.

She must have heard him, though, or felt the tension in him because she looked up to meet his gaze. "You're very lucky. This is one of his best." Her voice was husky. She seemed so vulnerable, almost overcome by emotion or maybe surprised—and not necessarily in a good way.

Trevor wanted to reassure her more than anything in the world. "I am very lucky," he murmured, and smiled down at her. "I met you."

He left her the choice, uncertain what she would do with it.

He hoped that she would touch more than his tattoo.

Chynna smiled and flushed a little, then reached up and touched her lips to his. Trevor had thought it might be a sweet kiss, or a dismissive one, but she angled her mouth over his hungrily. Her hands rose to his shoulders and she gripped him, pulling him closer as she feasted upon his mouth.

Relief surged through him.

If Chynna wanted a buffet, Trevor was hers for the taking.

༄

Chynna had almost lost her nerve.

She'd been surprised. Seeing those two koi by Tristan, one blue and one gold, swimming in opposite directions on Trevor's arm had taken her breath away. Chynna could have interpreted it as a sign that she was making a mistake.

But they were so beautiful, so perfect, so artfully drawn that she expected them to keep swimming and change places with each other. They were some of Tristan's best, and so she chose to see the presence of his work as encouragement. Tristan, after all, had told her to fall in love again, though she had known it would be impossible. He had insisted that she continue to live after he was gone, but really, she hadn't.

And these two beautiful fish reminded her of the promise she'd made to Tristan, the one she hadn't kept. She wasn't going to fall in love ever again— her heart had been surrendered forever to Tristan— but she could *live*.

She knew that Trevor was startled by her confession, but she touched him boldly and he seemed to forget the interruption. He let her set the pace but he responded with enthusiasm to every move she made. She caressed him, liking that he was so hard and thick, so ready. She liked how taut he was, how his body was like a work of sculpture. He took pride in his fitness and his appearance, and Chynna liked the result very much. He was strong and vital, powerful and gentle.

And he wanted her.

Under the Mistletoe

She backed him toward the bedroom, feasting upon his mouth, one hand locked around his neck and the other around his waist. His shirt was gone and his skin was warm and tanned. His hands were in her hair, cupping her head, as they kissed hungrily. When he backed into the door frame, he spun her around, breaking their kiss, and unzipped her dress the rest of the way. It slithered to the floor, the sequins gleaming, and she felt like a mermaid shedding her skin.

Her bra followed it and she saw him catch his breath. He smiled and cupped one breast in his hand, bending to kiss the nipple. Chynna watched him, her heart in her throat. It was easy to remember how showing her passion had excited Tristan and clearly Trevor felt the same way. She pulled his mouth back to hers and kissed him, her mouth open, her tongue demanding, and he moaned. The sound of his need enflamed her and made her want more. It made her impatient.

She urged him into the bedroom, its shadows illuminated only by the lamps in the other room. Even in the darkness, she could see it was tidy and simple, just a king-sized bed with two end tables and a bureau on the opposite wall. There was no clutter of possessions or laundry, no pictures to distract her, no television or clock. This room was more like a hotel room, anonymous and without distractions.

A veritable hotel room with a virtual stranger. She would never return to Honey Hill. She would never see Trevor again. Chynna could do what she wanted, when she wanted. She could act without repercussions or rumors or expectations. She felt gloriously unencumbered, free to give pleasure and accept it. This night would have no legacy.

It would be a new beginning.

The heart tattoo that Tristan had given her all those years ago burned like a brand.

Trevor's legs collided with the bed and Chynna ran her hands over him with possessive ease before she unfastened his trousers. His briefs followed and she caught her breath at the size of him, then she bent and took him in her mouth.

He gasped with pleasure, his fingers tightening in her hair. She loved that he was surprised by her move and teased him with her lips and tongue. He whispered her name, and Chynna caressed his balls, feeling his response to her moves. She was sure he was holding his breath, so taut with need, but then he scooped her up in his arms, pivoted and laid her on the bed. Her panties were gone and he bent down, his eyes gleaming with intent, his mouth closing over her, and it was her turn to gasp.

He was relentless, persuasive, persistent and completely seductive. Chynna surrendered completely to sensation, letting him pleasure her and wanting only more. He was playful and that made her smile, alternatively tender and demanding. He surprised her with a brush of his teeth or a flick of his tongue, and she'd had any inhibitions, they didn't survive long. She lost track of time and of every concern except Trevor's skillful lovemaking.

She heard her heart race. She felt her skin heat. She rode a tide of sensation, knowing she writhed on his bed, knowing she was incoherent in her demands, and loving every second of it.

And when her release came, it was joyous, jubilant, marvelous. She screamed aloud, as she never did, not caring who heard.

Trevor chuckled, a wonderful dark and sexy sound, then climbed up beside her. He wiped his mouth, his gaze devouring her. "Okay?"

Chynna was still catching her breath. "More than okay and you know it."

She could see his eyes gleam, even in the shadows. His smile was irresistible and she ran a fingertip across his mouth, watching her progress of her finger hungrily. When she reached to replace it with her mouth, he met her halfway, leaning over her as they kissed with the same heat as before. She could feel his erection against her hip and reached to caress him but he broke their kiss, shaking his head.

"Not now. I'm too close."

"But I've been ignoring you."

He inhaled and ran a hand over her. "The way you come is like magic." His hand closed over her breast and he pinched her nipple, rolling it between finger and thumb. Chynna arched her back as he watched her. "So beautiful, and so honest. That's good for me as well as you."

"Because you like to watch?"

"Because I like to make you come." He bent and

took that nipple in his mouth, tormenting it with his teeth and tongue so that Chynna was writhing on the bed in pleasure again.

"I'll come again," she whispered.

"Then scream again when you do," he murmured against her flesh. "Make all the noise you want."

"You don't mind?"

"I love it. It's like I've pushed you over an edge, like you can't help but lose control."

"I couldn't."

"Good. I love that." His hand slipped between her thighs, his fingertips brushing against her clitoris again. She was so wet, so slick with need, but all she could do was part her legs in silent demand.

"Hearing me come or making me lose control?" Chynna asked, her words breathless. She wasn't used to talking while making love. Tristan had always been intent but silent. She found it titillating in a way, and she liked that it made her more keenly aware that she was with Trevor, not Tristan.

Maybe that was his point.

Maybe he wanted her to be making love to *him* not to a phantom in her memories. Chynna had no quibbles with that. Trevor gave her all of his attention, as if determined to explore every inch of her, and she felt both admired and beautiful beneath his touch. His fingers were moving against her, his sure touch making her want to moan, then he slid two fingers inside her and Chynna did moan.

"More?" he asked.

Chynna nodded. "Oh yes," she gasped.

He smiled and eased another finger inside her, his thumb continuing to rub back and forth against her clitoris. Chynna grabbed his shoulders and hung on to him, letting her fingernails dig into him and watching him smile. "Hearing me come or making me lose control? Which do you love more?" she asked again.

"Both," Trevor whispered, abandoning her nipple to kiss his way to her mouth again. "I want it all," he whispered in her ear when he was looming over her, pressing her slightly into the mattress. "I want everything you have to give, Chynna. I want you to scream and shout and scratch my back and wrap your legs around me. I want you to ride me until dawn."

Chynna squirmed beneath him, mesmerized by his words and his touch. She seized a fistful of hair at his nape and arched her back to rub her breasts against his chest.

"Tell me what you want," he invited in a growl. "Tell me what you need."

"You," she confessed. "I want you and I want you now. I want all of you. I want it hard and I want it fast." He inhaled sharply and she smiled at him. "Then I want it slow, while I'm on top."

"Lady's choice," Trevor murmured and gave her clitoris a teasing little pinch. Chynna caught her breath, almost coming, but then he was reaching for the nightstand. He pulled out some condoms and she chose one, then eased it over him. He closed his eyes, savoring her touch, then he was over her and inside her, the size of him making her arch her back again and moan. He paused and she felt him studying her. "You're so tight," he whispered, strain in his voice.

"It's been a while." Chynna opened her eyes and smiled at him, liking that his hair was tousled and his gaze intent. "But definitely worth the wait."

"And now?"

"All of you," she said. "Fast and hard." She lifted her legs and wrapped them around his waist, watching him inhale sharply. She ran a hand over his tattoo, admiring it again. He surveyed her and shook his head, as if he couldn't believe that she was with him. "What do you want?" she whispered.

"You. Right here and right now." He bent to kiss her cheek. "With your eyes open."

It was fair, in Chynna's view. And because she was, she was happy to comply. She smiled up at him, winding her arms around his neck and drawing him closer for a slow, sweet kiss.

They moved together as if they'd been making love for years instead of mere moments, and he moved so that he rubbed against her just right. Their gazes locked and held, the heat rising between them as he moved steadily. Chynna was caught by surprise, the tide of pleasure surging through her with stunning power. She whispered his name and clutched his shoulders as she came in a rush. He roared as he buried himself deep inside her and came, shuddering with the power of his release.

Under the Mistletoe

They collapsed together, slick and hot, their breath coming quickly. She could feel his heart thundering where his chest was pressed against hers and she halfway thought their hearts were beating in unison.

Her heart tattoo was thrumming.

"Oh, Trevor," she whispered when he laid his head on her shoulder, his breath coming quickly. She stroked his hair and his back, feeling fortunate that she'd chosen such a thoughtful lover. "Thank you."

He braced himself on his elbow and smiled down at her, looking disheveled, pleased and very masculine. Her heart skipped and she felt self-conscious then, as if she'd made a mistake.

"Thank you, Chynna," he said, then stole a kiss. "Give me a minute before round two."

Chynna averted her gaze, not certain she could bear another round. How could she escape without insulting him?

Trevor felt the shift in Chynna's mood. Her eyes revealed her thoughts so clearly. He knew that this was an exception to her usual choices and had wondered why. Her reaction to his tattoo made it clear that she was mourning Tristan's loss, and he'd almost stepped away. He never wanted to be a stand-in for anyone else. Then she'd touched him so boldly, as if she was determined to propel them both onward, and he hadn't been able to resist.

He knew he'd pleased her. He knew she was

aware that he wasn't her former partner, because he'd made sure of it.

But now, he also knew that she was ready to run.

If he hadn't felt such a strong connection with her, he might have let her go. He might have made it easy for her, by pretending to fall asleep—or even really falling asleep. But Trevor wanted a genuine chance, and the possibilities of that would be improved if Chynna stayed.

If he forged an emotional connection.

He stood up and offered his hand to her. "So, tell me what you love best about what you do."

She eyed him for a moment, then put her hand in his. "Why?"

"I'm curious. What's the best part of being a tattoo artist?" He'd caught her attention and he knew it. He led her to the bathroom before she could change her mind, and turned on the shower.

"Thinking of changing careers?" she asked with a smile.

"No, I'm just always interested in why people do what they do. It's clear that you like tattoos and an admiration for the form might be part of it." He shrugged as he tested the heat of the water. "But it might be more. I'm thinking that it is, actually."

"Why?"

"I don't know. Just a feeling." He smiled at her and Chynna smiled back, then joined him in the shower. It was a great shower, in Trevor's opinion, tiled with large marble squares and easily big enough for two people. He was glad that his unit had this large walk-in shower instead of the tub and shower combination. The lodge also had good towels, great thick ones, and provided toiletries from a local artisan. The bathroom floor was heated, too, as well as the towel bars. Gabe understood that the spa experience was part of the appeal of a weekend retreat for many guests. Trevor had been the one to suggest they add two robes to each room. Guests could buy the robes if they liked them, and they'd already sold half a dozen.

Trevor worked up a lather with the body wash in his hands and began to smooth it over Chynna. "Full service?" she teased and he grinned.

"Consider me your slave of the moment."

She laughed. "Oh, that smells nice."

"Local. It's good stuff."

Her eyes sparkled. "And you sell it in the lobby."

"Of course. I told you Gabe was brilliant." He smiled at her and saw that she was less agitated. "Come on, indulge me."

"Didn't we do that already?"

"That was sensory indulgence. Tell me the best part of what you do."

"Tell you a secret," Chynna said, interpreting his question. She was watching him and he guessed that her secrets were closely guarded.

"Doesn't have to be. It might be your official answer, the one you give to school groups when you're invited to talk about your choice of career."

Chynna laughed again, surprised into it. "I don't get a lot of those invitations."

"Neither do I, actually. I think they all go to cops and veterinarians."

She laughed again, then sobered as she considered his question. "What do I like best about being a tattoo artist?" she mused as he washed her back. "Well, there are a lot of things. I like the artwork and how a similar design can look so different on different people." Her gaze dropped to his koi tattoo and he didn't want her thoughts to follow that direction, straight back to her dead lover.

"What else?"

"I like doing the work. It takes time and it's meditative, if the client isn't chatty. I can focus on creating the image on their skin and bringing the design to fruition." She nodded and took some body wash in her own hands, lathering it up. "I like that tattoos are art but not locked up in a gallery. They're visible everywhere the bearer goes."

"Art on the move."

"Art loose in the world. I like that people engage with the tattoos. They look. They ask questions. They want to touch them. If nothing else, the ink sparks their curiosity. They assume that the images have meaning and want to know more."

"They're conversation starters," Trevor agreed. "And mirrors of the soul."

"That's supposed to be eyes," she countered with a smile.

"It is, but I think people guess more about you from these roses than from the expression in your eyes at any moment."

"What do you think they guess?"

"That you're a romantic. That you're detail-oriented and private, too."

"How so?"

"The roses are perfect, which makes me think you were particular about them, but there are secrets hidden within them." He ran his hand over her arm. "I see dew drops and there's a spider here, plus a little fairy face there. Someone has to look closely to see all the detail, and might still miss some of it then. That makes me think you're a private person, one who doesn't put everything in the proverbial window or confide in just anybody."

She smiled, pleased.

"Your sleeves make me think that you're an artist, because they come together with a cohesiveness that must have been planned. So maybe it's been curated into coherence."

She smiled at that.

"That you have such extensive tattoos makes me think you must be a person who lives by her own rules. That you're concerned with beauty and visual effect, and that your definition of beauty might defy conventional expectation."

"That *is* a lot," she said, looking a bit startled that he'd gleaned so much. She was private, that was for sure.

Trevor took a risk then, in an attempt to put them on more even ground. "Go ahead. Play the game. Tell me what my tattoo makes you conclude about me." She studied the koi, her expression serious, and he watched her swallow.

He felt as if things hung in the balance, but he'd always been one to take the risk.

Chynna dropped her hands to his skin, rubbing the soap lather over the fish, then wiping it away selectively. "That you're discerning," she said finally.

"Why?"

"Because you only have one tattoo and it's a work of art." She frowned. "That you have some money because this size of tattoo is an investment. Tristan had a reputation and was expensive. That means you were committed to having it. It wasn't a whim. It took time, too. That probably indicates that you're thoughtful, and that you do a lot of research before making a decision. I doubt that you're changeable—you commit to a course and hold to it. A tattoo like this can't be undone. It can't be hidden either, so you're confident of who you are and don't worry about who sees your truth." Her gaze flicked to his. "How's that?"

"Windows to the soul," he said, stealing a quick kiss. He spun her around to give her a little shoulder massage. "So, that's what you love best about what you do? The visual experience?"

"No," she admitted, surprising him. "It's the people. I like that they come with their stories and their ideas and their needs and that they share all of that with me."

"Needs?"

"For many people, tattoos are cathartic."

"Like mourning tattoos," Trevor guessed. He wondered if that's what her roses were.

"Exactly. Those people talk during the work. They might tell me about the person or emotion that they want to commemorate. They might tell me about their loss or about their joy. Quite often, it's clear that they haven't talked to anyone else and so sharing the story helps them to heal. In a way, the tattoo becomes a living metaphor: as it heals, so do they. I like that a lot."

"So, that makes you a kind of councilor or healer."

She cast him a smile. "Not always, but sometimes. There can be a psychic exchange."

"That must be hard on you."

"It can be draining, but it's good work. We had a rule at Imagination Ink of doing only one memorial tattoo each per day. Sometimes even that was too much. But even when you're tired from sharing someone's pain, it's a good feeling. You know you helped, and maybe that makes the world a better place." Her gaze rose to his and he saw how deeply she believed this. "You feel like you made a difference, like it mattered, and that is a tremendous blessing."

Trevor nodded in understanding. He reached out and touched the tiny red heart tattoo on her throat. "Like these hearts, one of which is responsible for this wedding."

She nodded. "It's not the heart tattoo *per se*, at least I don't think so. It's that getting it makes the recipient reconsider his or her options, and maybe see something they overlooked before."

"Or decide to do something about a dream, like Liv."

"And Lexi, too. I felt that she needed a burst of confidence to reach for what she really wanted, and if the tattoo did that for her, it was a very good thing. The tattoo was a nudge. She had to do the rest herself."

"Did you go to her show in New York?"

"I did." Chynna's smile was radiant. "She's wonderfully talented."

"So, which one is your memorial tattoo?" Trevor asked and regretted the words as soon as they left his mouth.

Chynna spun to stare at him, eyes wide, then reached for the glass door. "None of them," she said, her tone clipped.

Trevor knew she was running this time and it was his own fault.

On the other hand, he had just about nothing left to lose. "Why not?"

She pivoted to face him. "Because I didn't want to surrender him," she said, her tone fierce. "I wanted to keep the memory close. It's *mine*."

Trevor watched her, knowing instinctively that this was only half of the story. "Don't you think you deserve to heal?"

Her eyes flashed before she turned her back on him and grabbed a towel. "I need to get some sleep if I'm going to sparkle tomorrow," she said, her tone more formal. "It's been a long day, but thank you for this interlude."

Trevor caught her shoulders in his hands. He felt her resistance and released her. "No second round, after all," he said, letting his disappointment show.

"The first time was more than good enough." She smiled but it was a polite expression and one that didn't light her eyes. He knew that she might as well already be gone. "Thank you."

"Thank you." Trevor knew when he was beaten. He let her go, giving her a bit of privacy in the bedroom to dress, taking a moment to brush his teeth. He left the bathroom wearing a towel around his hips, and arrived in time to zip up the back of her dress. He dropped a kiss to her shoulder, then slipped one of his cards into her hand. "Sleep well, and feel free to call if you need anything."

"Thank you," she said, then headed for the door. Trevor opened it for her and she shook her head.

"Always a gentleman? Or always serving?"

"The first in this case, although the second is often true too."

She nodded, met his gaze briefly again. "Thank you, Trevor," she said, her tone softer. "It was nice."

After she was gone, he leaned back against the door, thinking.

Once hadn't been enough for him, but in Trevor's world, it was always lady's choice. In this case, he'd pushed too hard and asked too much, letting his curiosity get the better of him, and he'd blown it.

If he had a second chance with Chynna—and that was a long shot—he wouldn't be so stupid again.

In between, he had Gabe's wedding to manage—in Trevor's mind, Gabe was the client, not the actual managing partner of the lodge. Everything had to be perfect in the next twenty-four hours, without the client's intervention or even knowledge when things went amiss.

It was a wedding. Things were going to go wrong.

Trevor would be on it, but even that challenge wouldn't be enough to keep him from thinking about Chynna. Didn't it just figure that he had offended the one woman to catch his eye?

Maybe he needed to cultivate a little of that mysterious air of hers. The idea made him smile again, because he was a straight-talker who always laid his cards on the table. Maybe he could hold back a bit.

It was worth a try.

CHAPTER THREE

Had she been rude?

Chynna had a hard time getting to sleep, despite being tired, and was up early the next morning. She made a cup of coffee in her room, tugged on the cozy robe supplied by the lodge, opened the drapes and watched the sunrise light the lake. There was frost on the window and snow on every surface. The lake was frozen, and she could see that an area near the lodge had been cleared of snow, as if people had been skating. The sky was cloudless and she watched it turn brighter blue as the sun rose. The ice glistened and it was a beautiful view.

Even better, she felt more attuned to sensation than she had in a while. Her room was warm and the coffee was delicious. The robe was thick and soft against her skin and she could remember the pleasure she'd felt the night before.

She'd felt admired and treasured. That was addictive stuff.

Maybe too addictive to indulge in just once.

She wrapped her hands around the warm mug, stared out the window, and had to think the morning would have been more perfect if she'd awakened with Trevor beside her. That was her own fault and she knew it. She could have stayed with him.

What was he doing this morning? What was he thinking about their time together?

Why had she run?

She'd become so good at building walls around herself to defend her grief and her privacy that Chynna wasn't sure how to begin to make a window in one—let alone a doorway—much less be certain whether she should. Did she want to be alone? Not really. Did she trust anyone enough to let them in? No. And Trevor was a poor candidate for that kind of a plan anyway. He lived in Maine. She'd never been to Maine before, would leave as soon as possible, and would never come back.

Still, he was more interesting than any man she'd met in years.

Chynna was sufficiently honest with herself to wonder if his unavailability for more than a day or two was part of Trevor's appeal.

Even so, her rudeness was inexcusable. He'd been a gentleman, but she'd practically left skid marks in her hurry to get out the door. Even though he'd shown an interest in her beyond the pleasure they'd shared together, she hadn't reciprocated. She knew very little about him, and even though that should have made it simpler to consider their night together a single event, Chynna felt that she'd been unkind.

Did he feel that she'd only wanted sex?

Did he feel used?

Could she do what she knew was right without putting her heart at risk? Chynna knew she invested too much too quickly with people. Tristan had always told her that, and had teased her about wearing her heart on her sleeve and giving people too many chances. But it was in her essence to give.

Trevor had asked her about Tristan. It wasn't an unfair topic of conversation, given his tattoo and her history. In a way, it showed that Trevor didn't just want a hook-up—and even if she did, Chynna liked that he was curious about more than her surface appeal.

Chynna couldn't let Trevor think that she thought less of him than she did.

It just wouldn't be right.

On the other hand, she'd never talked about Tristan to anyone. Maybe it was time. Maybe a man she'd never see again after this wedding was a good choice of confidante.

What if they shared another night? What if she ventured a little bit more? She knew the sex would be great and suspected that wouldn't be the sum of it.

She looked at the ring on the chain around her neck, her wedding ring, her mind filling with memories, bitter and sweet. It was time.

She showered and dressed, filled with new purpose. Instead of ordering room service for breakfast and hiding in her room, she went looking for food.

And Trevor.

She'd issue an invitation of her own.

There was no answer to Chynna's knock on Trevor's door. She wondered if she had the right door, but was sure it had been this one. She knocked again, aware of the silence of the corridor. If there were guests in the rooms that faced the lake, they were still sleeping.

And no wonder. It was early. The party had been a good one. She reasoned that most guests at the lodge were also attending the wedding, so would have been at the party the night before.

She went down to the restaurant beside the lobby, which was quiet too. There was a young woman on the front desk, who smiled at Chynna and greeted her.

"Is it too early for breakfast?" Chynna asked.

"There won't be a hot breakfast available until the brunch buffet opens at ten, but there's a complimentary continental breakfast for the wedding guests." The girl came out from behind the desk to show Chynna where it was laid out.

She followed the other woman into the

restaurant, not really surprised to find that she was alone. There was a tray of fresh fruit, attractively arranged, and a variety of breads, bagels, muffins and donuts. Chynna took a container of yogurt with a selection of fruit, and used the single serve coffeemaker to make herself a second cup.

"Good morning."

She jumped at the sound of Trevor's voice and turned to find him in the doorway. His hair was wet and his chest was bare, and he was just as trim and toned as she'd thought the night before. No illusions there. He could have been a professional athlete and she heated at the memory of his sculpted chest against her own. Her gaze lingered on the koi tattoo again, her chest tightening at the sight of Tristan's work, and she met his gaze to find him watching her, consideration in those dark eyes.

As well as a heat that made her heart skip.

Trevor was wearing a black swimsuit and flip-flops, and carried one of the hotel towels. He'd obviously been for a swim and she wondered if he knew he was standing under the mistletoe hung in the lobby.

She pointed at it and he tipped his head back. His smile claimed his lips slowly, lighting his features just the way the morning sun had lit the lake. When he met her gaze again, there was a fire in his eyes. Chynna felt warm. His smile hinted at an appreciation of what he saw. It was nice to be admired, and nicer yet to be admired by such a gorgeous man.

Even better, Chynna had to think she hadn't completely trashed their prospects, given the heat in his eyes.

"Should I move?" he asked quietly, his voice a low murmur.

Chynna swallowed. "Not on my account," she said and took a step toward him. She saw him catch his breath but he waited, not even blinking as she approached.

"Good morning," she said, then stretched up to brush her lips across his. She could have sworn her skin sizzled at just that brief contact and she felt him inhale sharply. She put her hand on his chest, unable to resist, and he made a low growl of satisfaction.

"I wish I wasn't wet," he said.

Chynna smiled. "Really? I'm glad I am."

Their gazes locked and held for an electric moment.

"Thank you for last night," she said finally. "It was great."

"It was. Thank you." He didn't move away yet didn't move closer either. He waited, watching, his body so tense that Chynna wanted to run her hands over him. She glanced beyond him but the lobby was empty, so she ran her hand down his chest to his navel, then back up again. When she looked up, his gaze was even more intent and his jaw was clenched.

"I didn't realize there was a pool."

He nodded. "Just ask at the front desk for the

key." She heard the tension in his voice, so stroked him again. She glanced down and saw his body's reaction to her touch, and smiled, liking that she could affect him so.

"No official hours?" She bent to touch her lips to his nipple and it tightened beneath her lips.

"No life guard." Trevor's voice was taut. "As long as you sign the acknowledgement of that, you can swim whenever you want."

"That's good to know. Thank you." She flicked her tongue across his nipple, then spared him a glance.

He arched a brow. "You look great this morning," he said as if she wasn't teasing him. "That bit of pink suits you."

"Thank you." Chynna had chosen the same pair of black jeans that she'd worn on the train the day before with a fuzzy hot pink sleeveless turtleneck. She'd pulled a black cardigan over that and worn her black boots. The only make-up she'd put on was her eyeliner.

"Do you often swim?" she asked and he grinned.

"I'd rather swim than lift weights," he admitted. "And getting some laps in early in the morning seems to work out better anyway."

"There will be lots to do, I guess, with the wedding."

"And so many of the staff are involved. I'll be picking up the slack today."

"You don't mind?"

He shook his head, resolute. "Of course not.

That's why I'm here."

Chynna frowned, her fingers stilling. "You're not always here?"

"No. I came to replace Gabe, but then he returned to the lodge because he and Lexi worked things out. I decided to stay on and help out for the festivities." Trevor shrugged. "It's good to see a friend happily in love."

"But you won't be staying at the lodge?"

"Only until they come back from their honeymoon."

"Will you stay in Maine?"

"I don't know." His sudden intensity made Chynna tingle. "It depends what opportunities present themselves." He watched her for a moment, as if waiting for an invitation, then changed the subject. 'Did you sleep well?"

"No," Chynna admitted.

Trevor nodded agreement. "Me neither." His gaze was searching.

"Even though I should have. It's like staying at a spa."

"They've got something good going here, that's for sure. I have a feeling that Gabe and Spencer will just go from success to success."

There was yearning in his tone and Chynna wondered at his own ambitions.

She took a breath and stroked her hand across his chest again. "I'm sorry I left in such a rush last night."

"I think it was this morning." His tone was

teasing, which was a relief.

"Either way, I was rude to you and that bothers me. I owe you an apology. I'm sorry. I ruined what had been a wonderful night."

"I don't think so." He shrugged and smiled, relief lighting his eyes. "I knew I'd hit a nerve. I apologize for being too curious. You just interest me and I tend to be direct."

Chynna decided to be blunt, too. "I felt like you wanted more than I'm ready to give."

"More being?"

"More than one night."

Trevor nodded and she liked that he didn't argue with her. "I am interested in more than a night, actually."

"But you don't know me well enough to be invested at all..."

"We could change that. We're both here."

"I'm not ready for more."

"Because of Tristan," he acknowledged, his gaze steady. "How long has it been again?"

"Ten years." It sounded like an eternity.

It felt like one, if Chynna was honest with herself.

"A decade," he echoed quietly. "When are you planning to be ready for more?"

"Maybe I'll just be alone for the duration."

"Because you believe that lightning only strikes once?"

"Yes. Of course. How could anyone expect more than one true love?"

Trevor pursed his lips, considering that. "I think you can expect anything, actually, and even better, that expectations often shape results."

"How so?"

"I never wanted to get involved with anyone until very recently." He looked into her eyes again, then captured her hand in his. His grip was warm and strong, but Chynna knew she could pull away if she wanted to.

She didn't. "What changed?"

"Maybe seeing Gabe so happy. I don't know." Trevor's thumb began to slide across her palm, feeding Chynna's desire for more. How could a man be so powerful and yet so tender? How could he be so patient? "I just became aware that something was missing in my life. I expected to fix that." His gaze locked with hers and he smiled a little. "And then you appeared. The first woman to intrigue me in a long, long time. Expectations shaping results."

Chynna couldn't help feeling flattered by that, even though she thought his logic was faulty. "Is it that or just your behavior? You could have met any number of women of interest and not noticed because you were focused on work. You could have missed a hundred opportunities."

That thumb moved relentlessly across her skin, feeding her desire for more. "Even if a person can expect only one true love in a lifetime?"

Chynna smiled. "Point to you."

"It doesn't really matter because the end result is the same. I'm interested in you." He studied her.

"No promises, no certainties, just curiosity. Who are you? What are we like together? Where will this go? Where could it lead? I want to know. Don't you?"

That he was so forthright surprised her but she liked it. She'd always admired honesty. Still, she didn't want to disappoint him. She knew she wasn't ready for more and she wouldn't mislead him. "The difference is that I don't think it can go anywhere and you obviously do."

"Because it already has," he countered. "Unless you've forgotten last night already."

"Of course not!"

"If that's the sum of it, I'll still be dreaming about you for a long time." He smiled. "Aren't you curious? You're here another day or two..."

"I leave tomorrow."

"So, what's the risk of a second night? Two nights instead of one. It's hardly a commitment for eternity."

"Then what is it?"

He shrugged. "An exploration?" His eyes started to twinkle, and she knew he'd guessed that she was on his side already.

Chynna shook her head, and teased him. "You don't give up easily, do you?"

"The secret of success in my world is persistence and planning."

"What are you planning?"

"Nothing yet. I'm still on the persistence part. Maybe I can convince you to grab this opportunity."

"To...?"

"To heal. To talk." He bent down to whisper in her ear. "To yell when you come." Chynna caught her breath but didn't step away. "To share some stories that need to be told, maybe stories you don't want to tell anyone you'll see regularly." His gaze held hers. "You can tell me anything. In a way, it's like a free pass. After you leave Honey Hill, we'll only see each other again if you invite me or make it happen. I'm not going to force myself on you. It's always lady's choice in my world. But why not seize the moment? There's some kind of intuitive connection between us and we can choose to enjoy it."

"For however long it lasts."

"Or for however long you're here. No strings attached."

"Why would you do that?"

His smile flashed. "Because I might even manage to change your mind." His eyes were sparkling as if he knew that wasn't likely.

"I'm going to guess you have a plan to go with that persistence."

"Of course. How about Twenty Questions?"

"I don't understand."

"We already did one informally: do you believe a person can have more than one true love? You say no and I say yes. So, let's go official. Ten questions from me and ten from you. We'll get through as many as we can before you head home."

"Okay. Who's going first?"

"Me. It's my game after all." He touched the tip

of her nose with one finger, still holding tightly to her hand. "Do you believe in love at first sight?"

"Yes."

"Me, too. Look at that." He raised that hand. "We have something in common."

Chynna smiled. "You're incorrigible."

"I try. I'm also getting cold and running late." He smiled at her. "Next question is yours. Make it a good one."

It was impossible to resist him. "Okay. I'm thinking."

He glanced up at the mistletoe. "Want to take advantage of this opportunity and maybe warm me up?"

"I already kissed you."

"That wasn't a kiss. Let me show you."

He waited until Chynna nodded, then wrapped an arm around her waist to pull her close. He smelled like his cologne and salt, so she knew it was a saltwater pool. She liked the strength of his arm and she liked the way he surveyed her, as if he couldn't believe his luck, before he slanted his mouth over hers and kissed her.

It was a kiss that refused to be ignored, one that heated her right to her toes, and made her stretch up to kiss him back. She wound her arms around his neck and opened her mouth to him, touching her tongue to his and savoring his little growl of satisfaction. His kiss made her forget that they were standing in the lobby, disheveled. It aroused her, and made her wish the day would fly by.

He lifted his head with obvious reluctance but didn't let her go. "I'll circle back to you when I can, but today is going to be insane for me."

"Well, it's going to be a challenge for me, too," Chynna admitted without intending to do so. There was something seductive about a free pass, just as he'd suggested.

"How so?"

"I haven't been to a wedding since Tristan died. I might completely fall apart."

Trevor sobered. "Need a volunteer to catch you?"

"Maybe a rock to lean on." There. She'd said it out loud. She waited to see what he'd do.

"I'll be there. I can be a good rock with the right motivation." Trevor winked and Chynna laughed a little.

Before she could thank him, the desk clerk called his name and Trevor glanced over his shoulder. His manner changed then, becoming more professional, as he released her. "Duty calls," he said with a smile that was cooler. Chynna distinctly felt that she'd become a guest again and she missed his avid interest. "It's time to get to it."

"Bring on the crises?"

"As few as possible, please, but some are inevitable. It is a wedding." He nodded, surveyed the restaurant as if checking that everything was in place, then pivoted and strode across the lobby. He spoke to the clerk at the front desk, then Chynna heard his footsteps on the stairs. It sounded like he took them two or three at a time. She felt cold in his absence but lighter inside.

She'd always liked mistletoe. Maybe she could catch him there again.

Chynna took her coffee and her breakfast to a table by the window and looked out at the lake. She was startled that he wouldn't be staying at the lodge for more than a month or so, but that still didn't mean she'd ever see him again. It was still a fling, and she decided to enjoy it. She'd warned him that she was leaving the next day.

She hadn't lived in the moment for a long time, even though it had once been her mantra. At this wedding, Chynna was going to fix that and get her life back.

She'd take Trevor up on that offer to listen. It might be just what she needed.

What would be her first question?

How was it possible for a woman to look so fabulously sexy and vulnerable at the same time? Trevor both wanted to scoop up Chynna, take her back to his room and ravish her again, and at the same time, to protect her from his own desire. And that kiss. She had the ability to make him forget everything, even work, which was a feat.

Maybe it was a sign.

Unfortunately this was not the day he could work on capturing her attention. If he had a chance to say more than three words to Chynna, Trevor would be surprised. His morning was off to a racing start and he couldn't resent it, because helping with the wedding was why he'd stayed in Maine—which had let him meet Chynna.

Murphy's Law always flourished at weddings, in Trevor's experience.

The first crisis erupted early but was addressed and potentially solved: the florists had declined to make the drive from Portland to deliver the flowers, citing concerns about the weather. Kade and Reyna had been coming into the lobby as Trevor fielded the call, transferring Reyna's wedding cupcakes to the lodge's refrigerator, and overheard. Kade offered to take Reyna's van down to the city and pick them up. The service was at two, which made the timing for Kade's drive a bit tight, especially if the roads were getting bad. There wasn't much Trevor could do about that, though.

His gut told him that more would go wrong and he was braced for it.

The bigger conference room had to be set up for the ceremony and fortunately, it wasn't otherwise booked. Liv and a woman from town were already decorating in there and their work might have to be enough if the flowers didn't arrive from Portland. Brunch had to be served in the restaurant and rooms had to be cleaned. One maid had already called in sick, so a replacement had to be found quickly. He'd asked the front desk clerk, Jenny, to make some calls as soon as she'd shared that news. They'd need every pair of hands they could get—and if they were short, he'd be refining his bed-making and toilet-cleaning skills. It wouldn't be the first time. The restaurant had to be changed around for the wedding reception after the brunch buffet, and more guests would be arriving at the lodge throughout the day.

Snow was forecast over Christmas. A lot of it, and the main snowfall was supposed to start the next day.

Trevor was striding down the hall, adjusting the knot in his tie and returning from the conference room to the front desk, when he saw that clouds were gathering over the lake. If that snow fell, people might end up staying longer than they'd planned: he needed to review the provisions with Spencer to make sure they could all be fed.

What if the power went out? Trevor decided to rent another generator, just in case.

Even as he hoped that guests weren't inconvenienced and all went well, a little corner of his heart hoped that Chynna did have to stay longer.

He wasn't quite ready to watch her walk out of his life, yet he knew that she wasn't anywhere near ready to let him be a part of hers.

Let it snow.

"I need another elephant," Lexi confessed. "Actually, I need two."

The bride-to-be had arrived with even more of a whirlwind that usual. She'd blown into the restaurant and caught Chynna up in a spiral of enthusiasm, then dropped into the opposite chair.

Lexi looked radiant, her eyes shining and her skin glowing. Her baby bump was big enough that it couldn't be hidden, but Lexi didn't even try. She was obviously one of those women who looked amazing during pregnancy and Chynna knew she'd never seen her looking better.

Happiness suited Lexi and Chynna was glad.

Lexi's hair had been cut short and given some highlights, and Chynna could see that it could look elegant if Lexi chose to bother. She was wearing jeans and a rugby shirt big enough that it might have been borrowed from Gabe. She wore no make-up but didn't need it at all. Her eyes were so striking, their pale silver-blue color making her more than beautiful. Heads would always turn when Lexi flew by. What Chynna loved was the sight of Lexi's confidence. She seemed to be brimming with it, and happiness, too—if Chynna had been any part of that change, she was glad.

The restaurant had become busier and the buffet was open. Chynna didn't know any of the other guests and she'd only caught a glimpse of Trevor in his suit, quietly ensuring that all went well. The mood was festive and they'd turned on the fairy lights that were strung from the ceiling of the restaurant. Chynna could smell bacon and she'd seen more than one guest take what looked like eggs benedict back to their seat from the buffet. Lexi's brother Spencer was busy, darting in and out of the kitchen, keeping a close eye on everything, and a trio of waitresses were keeping everyone's coffee cups filled. Chynna had been thinking about indulging in the eggs benedict herself when Lexi arrived.

"Another elephant tattoo?" she echoed mildly. "How big?"

"Did you bring your tattoo gun?"

"Chynna never goes anywhere without her favorite tattoo gun," Reyna said, taking a third chair at the table. She gave Chynna a hug and a kiss of welcome, even though they'd spoken the night before. In contrast to Lexi, Reyna's hair was perfectly arranged in a fifties up-do and she was fully made up. She was wearing a navy blue sweater dress that hugged her curves, along with spectator pumps in navy and white. Her nails and lipstick were a glossy soft pink. She might have looked like a movie star, except that the ink of her extensive tattoos peeked out from beneath her cuffs and was visible through her sheer stockings.

"You're right. I don't," Chynna said. "But you can't want to have this done today."

"I do!" Lexi said. "It has to be today."

"But your skin will be enflamed..."

"And I'll feel the burn of the new elephants as I'm exchanging my vows. It'll be perfect."

"I told you that you should have gone to New York to get it done sooner," Reyna chided. "Then it would have healed by now."

"But I wanted it to be today," Lexi insisted. "I wanted it to be part of today."

"Why?" Chynna asked.

Lexi leaned closer, her eyes shining. "Because *she's* coming, and I want her to see how much that matters to me."

She could only be one person. "Your daughter?" Chynna guessed and Lexi nodded.

"With her parents."

Chynna was glad that Lexi didn't distinguish them as being 'adoptive' parents.

Lexi sat back and squared her shoulders. "I've talked to them, and I talked to her a couple of times on the phone. They're coming from Boston but just for the day. They'll go back in the morning to have their Christmas at home."

"It's nice of them to make such a big trip."

Lexi nodded, her gratitude clear. "I want her to understand that she wasn't an accident." She took a deep breath. "I want her to know that Gabe and I had a powerful connection from the very beginning and that she's the result of that."

"You want to teach her the power of love," Chynna suggested.

"I think she knows it already. Her parents, Brad and Teresa, are awesome people and they've given her really good roots." Lexi shrugged. "I just think it can't hurt anyone to have a few more. They agreed."

"You didn't want to meet her before, and that wasn't very long ago," Chynna reminded Lexi gently. She didn't want to put a damper on the younger woman's enthusiasm, but felt the need to be sure there'd been enough thought behind the choice.

Not that she could do much about it either way.

"It was before I started to paint, though," Lexi explained. "It was before I worked through the bad stuff to find the good work again." She smiled. "And let's be honest. It was before I had a show that sold out, and found myself a career, the one I always wanted to have."

"But were afraid to reach for," Reyna supplied.

Lexi's gaze was steady. "I can be proud of what I'm doing now, and that means I can face her."

Reyna frowned thoughtfully. "Don't you think that part of what you want to teach her is that screwing up doesn't mean you have it wrong forever? That you can take a second chance at something if you believe in it enough, and make it happen?"

Lexi nodded. "Well, there's that, too."

"And that dreams don't have an expiration date," Chynna added. "The point is that you pursue them, whenever you do, even if you give up for a little while."

"That, too," Lexi admitted, then appealed to Chynna. "Will you do it today?"

Chynna finished her coffee and put the cup aside. She was unwilling to commit until she knew the extent of what Lexi wanted added to her tattoo. "Tell me about these elephants."

Lexi kicked off her shoe and pulled up her leg, displaying the pair of elephants on the side of her ankle. They were line drawings, nicely done but overly simple in Chynna's view. The red heart she'd added for Lexi, above the two entwined elephant trunks, was the only color in the vicinity. "This is me and this is my daughter."

"What is her name?"

"I didn't give her one, not then."

"But they must have."

Lexi eyed the tattoo, her lips pursed. "I halfway think that if I say her name out loud, it will jinx everything. They won't show up, or they'll change their minds, or somehow I'll lose her all over again."

"You talked to her," Reyna reminded her.

"Just short calls. They've been pretty awkward." Lexi shook her head. "None of that magical intuitive connection going on for us." She glanced at Chynna. "None of this is easy, but I know it's the right thing to do."

Chynna nodded, understanding that this was another thing Lexi wanted to share with her daughter.

"I have to show her that she matters to me, that I was trying to make the best choice for her, and with any luck a good one for me, too. I don't want her to think she wasn't wanted, or that she was thrown away. I wanted her with all my heart. I just knew that I wouldn't be able to do anything good for her."

"Maybe something," Reyna said, giving Lexi a nudge.

"But not everything. Not what she has now. I'm glad she has parents who love her and have given her so many advantages. I'd just like to know her a little bit, if she wants that, too." Lexi bit her lip. "In her place, I might not want to know me at all."

"And so the elephants," Chynna prompted.

"The elephants," Lexi agreed. "Because elephants remember, and I never forgot her. I never will, no matter how this works out, and I'll never stop wanting her to have every good thing in her life."

Chynna smiled.

"But there are other things I want to remember and commemorate. I'm not sure how to add them in, Chynna, but maybe you have a suggestion. I was thinking of adding a mirrored pair of elephants, with the two little elephants having their tails entwined."

"Kind of an elephant chain," Chynna said, turning Lexi's ankle to consider the canvas she had to work on. "The other big one would be on the front of your ankle then."

"Yes, I guess it would. So, there'd be me and Gabe and Kristen and the baby on the way. All of us connected, but each of us distinct."

Chynna nodded.

"What are you thinking?" Reyna asked in a wicked whisper. "I see those wheels turning, Chynna!"

"Do you really want my idea?" she asked Lexi. "Or is yours firm?"

"Tell me, please."

"I find the elephants very plain. That's okay. It's your choice. But if they're going to wrap around your ankle, it might be nice if they looked like jewelry."

"I don't understand," Lexi said.

Chynna glanced around for a pen and paper, but Reyna quickly produced both from her tiny clutch purse. "Always be prepared in the company of artists," she said, prompting both Chynna and Lexi to smile.

Chynna was already doodling. She drew the elephants that Lexi had already and added their mirror images, then began to create swirls around them. She thought of fences and copperplate curls on typography, as well as flourishes and embellishments in old books. She thought of henna tattoos and mandalas and the decorative hems on silk saris. The elephants ended up in an ornamental band that was about three inches wide

"It looks like wrought iron scrollwork," Reyna said, watching.

"Or an anklet of silver," Lexi said with excitement. "Put red hearts in it, like rubies."

Chynna added a heart between each pair of elephants, then drew a medallion and a flourish around each one. They wouldn't all be her magic hearts, but they still looked good.

Maybe the whole piece would be a talisman.

Lexi turned the drawing around to consider it. "They're individuals, but part of a herd," she said. "They have support from each other, and also from the filigree that looks decorative."

"Maybe it's tougher than it looks," Reyna suggested.

Lexi put her finger on the heart in the drawing that represented the one Chynna had given her on the full moon. "Maybe it's the magic of love," she said, lifting her gaze to Chynna's. "I love this. It's perfect."

"And it's too much work to do today," Chynna said, knowing she had to be realistic.

"I told you that you should have done this sooner," Reyna chided. "Good work can't be rushed."

Lexi wrinkled her nose at the truth of that. "Could you do the outline today?"

Chynna looked around, noting the number of guests gathered for brunch and saw more arriving in the lobby. She knew that it would be a busy day for Lexi and couldn't imagine the other woman had a lot of time to spare. "I don't think this should be rushed."

"Will you outline the new elephants?"

It was clearly important to Lexi to have this image for her wedding. "That I can do, but I'll have to do some preparations. What if we put the stencil on for the whole thing and I'll tattoo what I can? The rest will be visible, even if it's not permanent, and I'll keep the stencil for when we finish up."

"Thank you, Chynna!" Lexi's pleasure was undisguised. "Reyna's going to do my hair. She has to do it this morning, so she can set up the cupcake wedding cake this afternoon."

"It's going to take a while to get it just right," Reyna said.

"I know! And it will be amazing." Lexi smiled at Chynna. "I could come to your room in an hour."

"It'll take me a few minutes to get ready. That will be great."

"Excellent," Lexi said, just as a woman called a greeting from the doorway.

"Lexi! I hope the groom isn't going to see you here this morning. It would be bad luck." She was older than Chynna and dressed in a bohemian style, still wearing her winter coat and boots, with a colorful knitted cowl around her neck.

"Mom!" Lexi laughed and flung herself out of her chair toward the new arrival.

"Her mom," Reyna said in an undertone, then nodded at that woman's companion. "And her lover, the art goddess."

Chynna didn't need to be told that the slender woman in a dramatic black cloak was Katerina Mitz-Taylor. She'd seen the other woman in articles about the art scene in New York and knew she was a famous—and stylish—curator. Lexi's mother looked softer and less decisive and Chynna wondered at what they had in common. Opposites attracted, maybe. There was some warmth between Lexi and Katerina, perhaps because of the successful show Katerina had mounted for Lexi earlier in the year. Their stars were rising together, Chynna thought, which always drew people together.

"Don't tell me you're going to wear *this* for the wedding!" Lexi's mom said to her, drawing back to survey Lexi's shirt and jeans.

Lexi laughed. "I need to wear something to primp, Mom. Reyna's going to help me go glam." She turned and gestured to Reyna, who excused herself from Chynna. Chynna watched the group of women, the introductions and the body language. She was intrigued by their meeting but couldn't hear their words.

"Opposites attract?" Trevor said from behind Chynna and she turned to smile at him.

"I didn't realize you were there!"

His smile was rueful, his gaze darting over the restaurant. "This is the day that I need to be everywhere at once."

"I'll bet." Chynna didn't want him to disappear just yet. "Should I try the eggs benedict?"

"Absolutely. And I'll meet you at the pool tomorrow morning to burn off that bearnais sauce."

"I didn't bring a swimsuit."

"If it's early enough, that won't matter." They laughed together, then Trevor raised his brows. "Actually, there will be more calories than that to burn by the time Spencer finishes making his magic today. The prep work in the kitchen is amazing. He's really outdoing himself."

"I can't wait." Chynna touched Trevor's hand as he turned away and he glanced back her. "Is there a copier I could use?"

"In the office. Just tell them I said it's fine."

"Thank you!" Chynna stood up as another wave of guests came into the restaurant. "I'd better get some of those eggs while I can."

"Get the lobster ones," Trevor advised. "They're delicious and decadent."

His gaze met hers then, his expression so hot that Chynna shivered from head to toe. They stared at each other for a long sizzling moment and a jolt slid through her, leaving her hot and bothered—and more than ready for a second night.

Maybe she'd wake the neighbors tonight.

CHAPTER FOUR

Reyna knew a thing or two about the healing power of tattoos, and she was relieved that Chynna had found a way to start the one for Lexi. She'd known that Lexi should get it done in advance, but there was no changing her friend's mind once it was set on something. Reyna could understand the desire to commemorate this day with this work though.

She would get Lexi's make-up and hair done as quickly as she could, to leave Chynna as much time as possible. The wedding would be at two, with the brunch buffet remaining open until one so even guests who arrived late could get something to eat. She knew there was going to be some sorcery in the restaurant and kitchen to get Spencer's roast turkey dinner with vegetarian options ready for seventy-five guests for six.

She also knew it would be delicious.

She tried not to look out the window too often, because the clouds were getting darker and Kade still hadn't gotten back from Portland. She hoped he was okay, and hated that she couldn't phone him and risk being a distraction. Patience seemed elusive but she focused on Lexi's transformation.

When she added the last stroke of blush to Lexi's cheek, she stood back. "Now you can look." She'd had Lexi sit with her back to the mirror so she couldn't complain about too much make-up.

Lexi spun around to consider her reflection and her lips parted in surprise. "You are amazing," she said as she looked closer. "How can I look like I have no make-up on at all when you've been at it all this time?"

"The natural look isn't quite," Reyna teased.

"I look like me but better."

"You look beautiful, because you are," Reyna said and Lexi gave her a hug.

"Thank you so much."

"We'll do your lipstick after you get dressed," she told her.

"I hope Chynna's ready." Lexi changed from her jeans to a loose sleeveless dress so her jeans wouldn't touch the stencil, then tugged on Gabe's shirt and a pair of Uggs. "I look like my mom," she said with a laugh, then led the way to the room Chynna had been given.

The door was open and the maids had already cleaned the room. The drapes had been pushed back and the view of the snow-covered lake was both pretty and bright—so long as Reyna didn't look at the snow clouds. She feared the storm might have started earlier near the coast. Chynna had placed a chair by the window where the light was best and pulled on a pair of latex gloves when Lexi tapped on the door. They considered the stencil together and Lexi approved it, then Lexi kicked off her boot and Chynna carefully applied the stencil to her ankle. Lexi was watching and talking quietly to Chynna about the placement. Reyna stood back, closer to the door, just worrying about Kade—until she felt someone's presence behind her.

A girl of maybe ten years old stood there. She had Lexi's dark hair, but her neat appearance was the very opposite of Lexi. Her eyes were dark, like Gabe's, and there was something of his serene confidence in her manner. A woman stood behind her, one hand on her shoulder, and they were both dressed both well and conservatively.

They hesitated together, watching Chynna and Lexi, who were unaware of them.

"You must be Teresa," Reyna said and offered her hand. "I'm Reyna, Lexi's friend."

"I am. How nice to meet you." Teresa was probably a few years older than Reyna but could have been from a different planet. She hid her surprise well when she took Reyna's hand, but couldn't keep herself from a quick survey of Reyna's ink and her rockabilly style. "And this is Kristen."

"It's good to meet you, too," Reyna said, shaking

the girl's hand. "I'm really glad that you were able to come today."

Teresa smiled a little, her gaze dropping to Kristen. "Kristen wanted to come. We'll head back to Boston in the morning and have Christmas at home."

Reyna nodded, well aware that Lexi and Chynna had realized they had company. Chynna smoothed the stencil in place, then straightened and stepped back.

Lexi rose to her feet, looking awed and uncertain. "Hi," she said finally. "Thank you for coming." She swallowed. "And thank you, Teresa, for making it possible."

The two moms smiled at each other tentatively. They were both uncertain but their love for this girl had brought them together.

"This is Chynna," Reyna said, moving into the room, hoping to encourage Teresa and Kristen to do the same. "She's from New York and has done most of my tattoos."

"Hello. I hope you had a good trip." Chynna removed her glove to shake hands with both of them.

"We made good time," Teresa said. "They forecast snow, but since it hadn't started yet, we decided to come."

"Now they say it'll be tomorrow," Lexi said.

Kristen had moved to look at Chynna's tattoo gun. She'd brought it in the stainless briefcase that she always carried, the one with foam inserts to securely hold two of her guns as well as ink and other supplies. The girl was evidently fascinated.

"Have you seen a tattoo gun before?" Chynna asked and Kristen shook her head. Chynna put her glove back on and explained how it worked, filling what might have been an uncomfortable situation. Lexi sank back into the chair, watching and listening. Chynna showed her the stencil and explained the process, and Teresa stood beside her daughter, listening.

"But you have a tattoo already," Kristen said to Lexi, indicating the elephants.

"I do. We're going to add to it today, because I want it to be about the future."

The girl frowned and really resembled Gabe. "It has a meaning?"

"Tattoos often have personal meanings," Chynna said. "Sometimes people get a tattoo to commemorate something or someone, or to indicate a change in their lives. It can be a change of perspective, or a fresh start, like a wedding or a graduation. A tattoo can be a reminder or a sign of membership in a group or even a means of attracting a certain kind of energy."

Kristen eyed Chynna's tattoos. "Is it rude to ask what they mean?"

"No, not really, so long as you respect that some people want to keep the meanings of their tattoos private."

"Do you?"

Chynna smiled. "I'll give you a short version.

Once upon a time, I was very much in love with a man who was also a tattoo artist. We were partners and then we were married and when he died, I felt more alone than I'd ever felt in my life. Another friend of mine gave me the roses so I'd remember the power of that love."

"But not him?"

Chynna's smile turned sad. "I'll never forget him."

"What about you?" Kristen asked Reyna.

"I'm one of those people who keep their secrets," Reyna said and the girl nodded.

She slanted a glance at Lexi, then back at the stencil, and Reyna recognized that this was the question she really wanted to ask. "What does yours mean?" she blurted out, again flicking a look at Lexi. "And why are you changing it?"

Lexi swallowed and looked down at her tattoo. She traced the shape of the elephants with a fingertip, and her words were husky when she spoke. "This is me and this is you," she admitted. "I chose elephants because they never forget."

"You thought you would forget me?"

"I knew I never would." Lexi looked up at her daughter. "I was hoping we'd have a chance to talk about this one day, but maybe we should do it right now. Maybe we need to do it right now." She didn't move but she kept her gaze on Kristen. "When I found out that I was pregnant, I made a choice. I thought I couldn't tell anyone about my pregnancy, because I was afraid of what they might say or do, so I chose to keep it secret. In the end, that just meant I was alone. I could have told my brother, Spencer. In fact, he asked me a lot of times what was wrong, but I was sure he wouldn't understand. I could have told my mom, but she was in the middle of a divorce from my dad, and I didn't think she had time for me. I was wrong. She would have made time for me." Lexi shook her head. "I would never have told my dad, though, and that was a good choice."

They smiled at each other.

"But I was alone because of my choices, and that meant I had to think of the future. I might not have planned to conceive a child, but once I was pregnant, I wanted to have my child. I wanted to have you. I wanted to keep you and raise you, and watch you grow up. I didn't want to miss one moment of your life." Lexi blinked back her tears, and traced the outline of the smaller elephant. "I wanted you to have everything," she said with heat. "But I couldn't give you much of anything." She raised her gaze. "I gave you up because I loved you, not because I didn't. Because I loved you so much, I let you go."

Kristen sniffled and Teresa gave her a tissue. She looked to be blinking back tears of her own.

Lexi took a shaking breath. "And because the one thing I could do for you was choose your parents, I was pretty relentless in researching the candidates."

"There's an understatement," Teresa said, with

laughter in her tone.

The two moms smiled at each other. "I'm really glad that Teresa and Brad put up with me and kept answering my questions. I knew that day when you were born and they came to the hospital, when I saw them even though I wasn't supposed to, that they were going to be the most awesome parents. I hope you agree that I picked well."

"I do," Kristen said, her voice shaky.

"Good," Lexi said. "We agree on something important, then."

Kristen laughed a little and some of the tension slid out of Teresa's stance.

Lexi turned to the stencil and indicated the other big elephant in the stencil. "See, this is Gabe, the man I love more than life itself, the man who is your father. I think we recognized something in each other from the first moment and knew we'd found our soul mates."

"And that's your baby," Kristen guessed.

Lexi nodded. "And this is the way we connect to each other and to the world, the way we support and encourage each other, the way we reach out to make families of choice as well as families of blood." She swallowed again. "I think the very worst thing was feeling so alone, not knowing what to do and not trusting anyone enough to ask for help. I hope that if there's one thing I can give you, it's another person to call. No matter what you do, no matter what happens, no matter where you are or when you feel alone, I'll listen. You don't have to take my advice or agree with any solutions I suggest, but you can always call and I'll always listen. I want to give you the belief that you'll never be alone, Kristen."

"Thank you," Kristen said quietly, and Reyna guessed from Lexi's dawning smile that Kristen was smiling at her.

Lexi exhaled. "So, we did that part and I feel better. How about you?"

Kristen nodded. "Can I watch you get the tattoo?"

"I won't get all of it today, just a little bit." She glanced at Chynna who looked at her watch.

"How about the outline of the other big elephant?" she suggested.

"For Gabe," Lexi agreed, her eyes lighting with love. "Yes, please." She looked at Kristen, obviously intending to make an impulsive suggestion. "We don't have many attendants today. No bridesmaids or ushers. Reyna is my maid-of-honor, and Spencer is standing up with Gabe. Would you—" she dropped her gaze and took a breath before looking at Kristen again. "Would you consider bearing the rings for us? You don't have to, if you'd rather not, but since you were part of the beginning for Gabe and me, I'd love it you were part of this day, too."

Kristen turned to look at Teresa.

"It's your choice, honey," Teresa said softly.

"I would like that," Kristen said to Lexi and Lexi rose from the chair, her eyes alight.

"Thank you!" she said, but stopped short of

embracing her daughter.

Kristen took a step closer. "What should I call you?"

"Whatever you want. You have a Mom already. How about Lexi?"

"Okay, Lexi," Kristen said, then reached out to touch Lexi's hand. They eased closer, studying each other, and then Kristen moved to give Lexi a hug. Lexi hugged her back, two tears of relief slipping free of her lashes. Reyna saw Teresa wipe her eyes, then made a joke to lighten the mood.

"Thank goodness for waterproof mascara," she said brightly and Lexi laughed as she stepped back. "Don't wipe!" Reyna scolded, then moved to dab Lexi's tears. "You'd better let Chynna get started or you won't even have that outline done."

The women laughed together and Kristen pulled up a chair to watch Chynna work. Reyna left with Teresa when the other woman went to their room to unpack. Reyna headed for the kitchen to put the finishing touches on her cupcakes. She felt shaky but relieved.

"All good?" Gabe asked in an undertone when she came out of the walk-in fridge with the first load.

"Kristen's going to be your ring bearer."

"Excellent!" Gabe's pleasure was obvious. "And Lexi's okay?"

"They're both great. She said what she wanted to say and it went really well."

"Good." Gabe exhaled. "Kade called," he said

and she spun to face him, fearing the worst. "He wanted to know if we needed anything else, because he said once he gets to the lodge, he's staying put. He's in Honey Hill. I told him to get his butt back here."

"Thank you!" Reyna put down the tray of cupcakes before she dropped them in her relief. Her hands were shaking, which was a sign of how much this man meant to her. "I know you can't see the bride today, Gabe, but why don't you have lunch with Brad, Teresa and Kristen? Kristen is watching Lexi get her tattoo and Teresa is unpacking, but after that drive, they'll all need to eat before the service."

"I'll talk to Spencer about keeping the buffet open for them," Gabe agreed and headed off with purpose.

"Good plan," Trevor said from the other side of the kitchen. Reyna hadn't realized he was there. "It's always good for the groom to have something to do."

She laughed. "You could give him one of your jobs today."

"I could, but I'm being too much of a control freak. Besides, Kade picked up the slack on the tough one. Did Gabe say he was in Honey Hill?"

Reyna nodded.

"Moments away, then. Good." Trevor sobered, focusing on the business at hand in a way that Reyna appreciated. "How do you want to set up the cake? I had a trolley left for you, but am not sure it's big enough for your display. Would you rather have a table set aside now, maybe with a curtain around it..."

The wedding venue was gorgeous.

Chynna had the privilege of just sitting back to watch the festivities unfold, since she had no part to play herself. She was glad that she'd gotten the outline done on Gabe's elephant in time and could enjoy being a guest.

She wasn't sure she would enjoy it, actually. This was the first wedding she'd attended since losing Tristan, by choice, and weddings always made her remember her own special day of making her vows to him. It was nearly Christmas, too, and she'd been honest with Theo about how difficult the holiday season was for her. She squared her shoulders and reminded herself that it was past time to join the living again.

The room set up for the service was a conference room, just down the corridor from the restaurant. One long wall was all glass windows and doors, overlooking both that long deck and the frozen lake beyond. In contrast to the cozy atmosphere of the restaurant, this room was brighter and simpler, with a high ceiling. With the decorations, Chynna could easily think of it as sacred space. The decor was wintery but not Christmas-y, which she hoped would make the wedding easier. Chynna would have named the theme "winter wonderland," and there was a lot of silver.

The chairs had been arranged in rows with an aisle leading toward the windows. Tree branches had been painted white and silver, then arranged to make a bower against the windows. The branches were adorned with fake snow and clear icicles, wound with fairy lights and hung with white and silver ornaments—many of fanciful snowflakes. There were a lot of evergreen boughs arranged in clusters with pine cones, and Chynna could smell both eucalyptus and lavender. There were touches of blue, teal and purple in the decor, but the silver and white were predominant.

There were silver lanterns lining the aisle, one at the end of each row of seats, with a fat beeswax candle burning inside. The aisle had a white carpet and a garland was draped from chair to chair on either side. The chairs all had silver slipcovers. There were fairy lights strung everywhere and the entire room glittered.

Snow was falling lightly beyond the windows, not yet accumulating very much. A pianist and a harpist played a duet and Chynna thought it was just perfect. Everything sparkled and there was an air of excitement. Chynna took a seat at the end of the second row, leaving the closer ones for family.

She saw Trevor quietly lighting the last of the candles and ensuring that everything was right. He spared her a wink but didn't stop to talk. She thought about their night ahead and anticipation flooded through her. Liv came to sit beside her and

Chynna noticed the silver ring on her left hand when it caught the light.

"Is that new?"

Liv's cheeks turned pink when she smiled. "Yes."

Chynna smiled. "Am I right to guess that Spencer has one, too?"

The younger woman nodded and showed Chynna the ring. "His is a little thicker. See? It has bees. He saw them and just knew I'd love them."

Of course. "When was the big day?"

"Friday, the day before yesterday. We wanted to do it quietly and not steal any of Lexi's thunder. This is her big day and she's waited for it."

"What about you?"

"I just wanted my mom there, and she was. My brother Brandon and I were never very close, and I couldn't see a good reason to spend so much money on a service. Spencer's family are all here for this one so we can share the news with them later today."

"You didn't want to be the bride at the middle of it all?" Even as she asked the question, Chynna thought she knew the answer. Liv tended to retreat from the spotlight so she might not enjoy being the focus of a big wedding. And Chynna wondered whether Spencer's partnership in the lodge meant that he didn't have a lot of spare cash. He was a practical person, too, and Chynna guessed that this pair would want to use the money for an investment in more than one beautiful day.

Liv shook her head. "I just want to be with Spencer forever. Thank you for convincing me to take a chance."

"You're welcome."

"I thought I only wanted one night, but he convinced me to dream of more." Her smile was filled with love. "I would never have known without your help."

Chynna reached over and gave Liv a hug, then had a closer look at her ring as she considered her words. The bees were cleverly done, just a few strokes of engraving that perfectly conveyed their essence.

How interesting that Liv had only wanted a night, but Spencer wanted more. She knew that Reyna had only wanted a night but Kade had convinced her to make a more permanent connection. And Lexi had been rootless since her single night with Gabe, years before, convinced that she would remain that way for good. It was impossible not to think of Trevor's hopes, and to wonder at her own prospects.

Then she wondered about her own secret heart tattoos. Maybe they did carry a little bit of magic of their own. Maybe they opened the recipient's eyes to a truth unnoticed.

Still, she couldn't believe it would work the same way for her. She had the original secret heart tattoo, the one that had brought her together with Tristan. It couldn't work again. She wouldn't want it to.

"When are you going to tell everyone?" she

asked Liv, wanting to still her thoughts.

"Maybe later tonight." Liv smiled. "Maybe not until tomorrow."

"A nice Christmas present?"

"The very best one." Liv was clearly happy and Chynna was fiercely glad to have played even a small part in that.

The music became a little louder then and the last of the guests hurried in to take their seats. Gabe and Spencer were first down the aisle and took their places in the gazebo. Both were wearing dark suits with white shirts and looked elegant. The officiant was a woman in flowing white robes who joked a little with Gabe, prompting him to smile. Trevor appeared out of nowhere with Kade, and Kade took a box to Gabe and Spencer. There were boutonnieres inside, each with a white rose and a sprig of evergreen, tied with a silver and teal ribbon. The officiant helped to pin them to their lapels, showing a knack with the task that the men lacked. They all chuckled together at that and Chynna wasn't the only guest who smiled as she watched.

The first row of seats were claimed by close family: Lexi and Spencer's mom and her partner were seated there, as well as an older gentleman with a younger woman who Chynna didn't know. There was a gap between the two couples, though they both sat on the bride's side.

Liv leaned closer and whispered. "That's Lexi and Spencer's dad and his wife, Gillian," she explained. "They only just arrived but I'm not sure they're staying for dinner."

Chynna felt her brows rise but she didn't say anything.

"They don't spend much time here," Liv said.

A pretty woman sat in the first row on the groom's side with another man and two kids. Kristen's parents sat beside them and they'd been chatting.

"That's Gabe's ex-wife, Daphne, with her partner Ned Wilcox and his kids, Cameron and Grace. I'm so glad they're here."

"You didn't think they would be?"

"It's a long way from New Mexico, but I was hoping they'd want to see the end of the story."

Chynna smiled at that. "A perfect ending."

Liv nodded happy agreement as the music changed. Her gaze was fixed on Spencer and Chynna noticed that he glanced at his new bride more than once. Kade took the seat beside Liv and Chynna was pleased when Trevor appeared beside her. He gave her a quick smile as he claimed the end seat in the row and she was impressed that he had made time to be with her.

He looked unshakable and reliable, and she almost smiled to think of him as a volunteer rock.

"How are the crises?" she asked in an undertone.

"Under control," he replied and gave her hand a squeeze. She guessed from his expression that he was juggling a lot and saw him check his watch.

But he'd kept his word to her. This man would be easy to get used to—unless, of course, he was on a mission and once he was on to the next one, his previous quests would be forgotten. Chynna wondered about his attention span then. Maybe she was just his current fascination.

He glanced down at her. "How about you?"

Chynna smiled. "Better than expected, but the music will get to me. It always does."

Trevor nodded and closed his hand more tightly over hers.

A hush fell over the guests as the music changed to the *Wedding March*. The music sent a predictable thrill through Chynna, but also made her heart tremble in exactly the way she'd anticipated. She and Tristan had gotten married at City Hall, but there had been a boombox and that song. Had he really been gone ten years? It seemed like yesterday that she'd been a nervous bride. The guests all stood and turned to look at the doorway, and Chynna was glad of Trevor's strong grip. She felt in need of a little support.

Kristen appeared first, her concentration fixed upon the purple velvet pillow she carried. Two golden rings gleamed against the dark velvet. The dress she'd brought to wear to the wedding was pink, but it matched everything well enough. Chynna saw Teresa smiling with pride. Kristen stopped in front of the officiant and that woman smiled at her, then said something quietly. Kristen beamed and moved to stand in front of Gabe.

Reyna was next, elegant in a silver dress and heels. The dress was sleeveless, but then had a fitted overdress in sheer matching chiffon, which both showed her tattoos to advantage and muted their color. She carried a bouquet of white roses mixed with evergreen and eucalyptus, trailing with silver and teal ribbons. She gave Gabe a kiss on the cheek, then took her place and turned to watch for Lexi.

All the guests caught their breath as one when she appeared.

Lexi was a beautiful bride, but Chynna hadn't expected otherwise. Her dress was surprisingly traditional in cut, fitted through the bust, long-sleeved and trailing across the carpet behind her. It was made of layers of chiffon and she looked as if she floated down the aisle. The unusual thing was the color of her dress—most of the chiffon was in shades of silver and grey, except for the topmost layer, which was teal. Lexi wore a tiara that sparkled in the light and no veil. She looked like a fairy maiden stepping down to earth, just for Gabe. Chynna glanced his way and saw his awe, knowing that Lexi's joy and Gabe's wonder were a perfect recipe for their future happiness.

When they all turned to face the silvery bower, Trevor captured Chynna's hand in his and didn't let go. She didn't really hear the greeting of the officiant but sat down with the other guests, a lump in her throat. She was fighting her tears, but they were tears of happiness, not as much of pain as she'd feared they would be.

She remembered her own wedding day.

She remembered seeing Tristan waiting for her

and how tightly her heart had clenched at the sight of him.

If she had known how few years they'd have together, she wouldn't have changed one thing. His love had been glorious and their happiness had been a gift unexpected. She was glad she had known him and glad he had loved her and it was only natural that she missed him with all her heart and soul.

But Trevor's grasp on her hand reminded her that life went on. There would be other celebrations and other joys, and Tristan himself had urged her to continue to live. Chynna took a deep breath as Lexi and Gabe exchanged their vows and interlaced her fingers with Trevor's. His interest in her was another gift and one she was going to appreciate. She'd be going home the next day, but would make their second and last night together something to remember.

Chynna was trembling.

Trevor would never have guessed by looking at her, but he could feel the slight shaking of her hand. That only meant he wasn't going to let go. He sensed that she was drawing strength from him, and thought it was maybe like the pain of getting a tattoo helping someone to move through their grief. If she and Tristan had been married, this service would remind her of their exchange of vows. Even if they hadn't technically been married, watching two people express their love to each other would evoke powerful memories.

He was more than glad to help her through this day.

He'd seen futures built on smaller foundations than that, and dared to hope.

He had to make sure everything was right for the reception, but he'd coax Chynna to smile before he left her. When the bride and groom kissed, he leaned down to murmur to her. "Do you think true love lasts forever?"

"It's not your turn," she whispered, fighting a smile already.

"I'm not really good at following rules."

"Me, neither," she admitted with a wicked little smile that made his heart skip a beat.

"Something else in common," he teased and her eyes sparkled.

"Relentless," she whispered.

"Probably my best quality. Persistence under another name."

She shook her head then considered Gabe and Lexi. "Why do I feel like that's a trick question?"

Trevor shrugged, striving to look innocent.

She laughed a little and nudged him. "Because it is. Okay, I still say yes. You?"

"No." He watched her eyes widen with surprise, then bent to whisper in her ear. She smelled fabulous and his grip tightened on her hand without him intending for that to happen. This lodge needed more mistletoe. "True love lasts forever if it's nurtured, but not if it's ignored or denied. It can't survive in a vacuum."

Chynna nodded slowly. "That's a good answer."

"Thank you." He let his tone turn teasing. "You really need to catch up here. I can't play this game alone. It's no fun."

"But you look like you're having fun."

"Do I?"

She met his gaze and that sizzle started again. She laughed and he squeezed her hand before releasing it. "All right. I will. Don't you have work to do?"

He blew her a kiss from his fingertips, drank in the sight of her smile, and headed back to work.

He liked that he could feel her watching him.

He liked the sense that he was on track to his goal.

He also liked that it had started to snow.

Kade didn't miss the flash of silver on Liv's left hand.

It hadn't been a great drive to Portland and back, but it had been better than he'd expected—the roads had been slippery—but the flash of relief in Reyna's expression when he walked into the lodge, burdened with flowers, had been worth every tense second.

Seeing Liv's ring made him aware that Reyna was standing up for Lexi, who was getting married, and that Liv, the third of the threesome of friends, had apparently also quietly tied the knot. He could see a silver band on Spencer's left hand, too.

He didn't think that Reyna would believe herself

Under the Mistletoe

to be left out—she wasn't one for following the crowd—but he didn't want her to have any doubts about his feelings or his hopes for their shared future. They'd bought real estate together, which indicated permanence, and shared both vehicles and beds, but he wanted more.

Was it too soon for Reyna?

He'd planned to ask her to marry him on New Year's Eve but as he watched the service and the woman who held his heart, Kade decided there was no time like the present.

He'd ask her before the day was through. It might have been nice to be sure of her reply in advance, but then she wouldn't be Reyna, the queen of surprises who kept him on his toes. That she could surprise him was part of the reason he loved her, and Kade wouldn't have her change for anything.

Not even him.

Chynna could only admire how smoothly the wedding guests were guided and managed. Trevor had vanished, but she liked that he had teased her before going back to work. He was thoughtful in ways she didn't anticipate. Now that the service was over, she felt more like her usual self.

The guests were invited back to the restaurant, some of them already having followed the sound of popping corks. Trevor was opening bottles of champagne at the bar. A waiter was pouring glasses to the brim with the bubbles and two others were circulating with trays. There were platters of crackers, cheese and fruit laid out for nibbling.

The tables were set and the room decorated in similar style to the wedding chapel. Tables were arranged for four or six guests and draped with silvery cloths. There were flowers on each table, with sparkly snowflakes in each arrangement, and glittering favors at each place. A silver lantern with a burning candle inside had pride of place on each table. Once again, there were fairy lights everywhere and a view of the lake. Fires were roaring in the fireplaces. A hostess with a list of the seating arrangements moved through the crowd, ensuring that the guests knew where they were to be seated.

At the far end, the wedding cake was displayed and Chynna went with Liv to admire it. It was on the top tier of a display taller than any Chynna had seen before. The cupcakes were topped with swirled teal or white icing, silver sparkles, and snowflakes made of icing. There were six layers of them, then a small cake on the top tier, also decorated with snowflakes and topped with a bride and groom.

"She matched Lexi's dress!" Liv said with delight.

"It's too pretty to eat," Chynna said.

"But it's going to be delicious," Liv said. "I just know it."

"The teal ones are chocolate," Kade supplied and Chynna turned to find him behind them. "And the white ones are lemon."

"Variety is the spice of life?" Liv asked and he

smiled.

"They couldn't decide on just one flavor so Reyna said she'd make both. And the cake is traditional fruit cake. They'll cut it later." He smiled. "I've heard *all* the plans."

The happy couple had gone outside for pictures in the snow. Several guests went out on the deck to take pictures of their own, and Chynna had a peek at the proceedings. It was chilly, though, and she didn't have a fur wrap like Lexi and Reyna.

They came along the deck then through the big doors into the restaurant to join the party, a dusting of snow on their shoulders and shoes. They accepted good wishes from the guests and glasses of champagne just as Chynna realized that Trevor had disappeared again. Chynna saw Spencer shed his suit jacket on the way to the kitchen. Within moments, she could smell warm hors d'oeuvres being prepared. She was to sit with Liv, Kade, and Jane, the woman who kept the bees in Honey Hill, for dinner and felt as if she'd be amongst friends.

A few guests looked out the window and made their excuses. Lexi's dad was the first to go, but Chynna saw that no one had expected differently. Lexi was obviously disappointed when Teresa and Brad decided to head back to Portland for the night, but encouraged them to leave sooner rather than later if that was their intention.

Chynna was glad to see Kristen give both Lexi and Gabe a hug, then Teresa and Lexi embraced and the men shook hands. Lexi looked shaken as she watched them go, but then she turned and gave Gabe a brilliant smile.

It had gone well, then. Chynna decided she'd suggest to Lexi that they invite Kristen to watch the completion of her tattoo. She thought of Theo with Tristan then, wondered if the bird had been a pest, and checked her phone for the first time in hours.

She found notifications for the holiday pop-ups for Flatiron Five, and smiled as she watched Theo and Kyle do their competitive lip-syncs, Theo in Manhattan and Kyle in San Francisco. They looked like they were having fun, and she was glad that Theo was stepping out of his comfort zone. She sent him a quick message, congratulating him and asking if Tristan was behaving himself, then smiled at the quick reply.

The raven was consistently stealing Theo's silver cufflinks.

Chynna typed a promise that she'd make sure Theo got them back. She put her phone away, still smiling, and looked around the room. She'd helped three couples find love and knew that Theo was making changes that could only lead to his own happiness, too. The little heart that Tristan had given her, the very first one, felt warm and she took that as a sign that she should reach for a little more happiness herself.

Another night with Trevor was the perfect plan.

CHAPTER FIVE

That smile.

Chynna had been talking to someone she loved. Trevor knew that smile and recognized its importance. One thing was for sure: he was never going to be a placeholder for some other guy. He'd made sure that Chynna knew she was with him the night before and he'd do it again.

He managed to work his way toward her with the bottle of champagne and offered to top up her glass. She smiled and turned her phone. "My crazy bird," she said, playing a short video of a black bird hopping on a coffee table. There was the sound of music in the background and tapdancing.

"Is he dancing along to something?"

"To a Fred Astaire movie. They're his favorites."

Trevor could only chuckle at that. "He does look like he's having a blast."

He filled up her glass, and she stopped him with a touch. "My turn," she reminded him, watching him. "What gives you the most joy?"

Trevor surveyed the room, calculated how much time he had, then knew the answer. "Easy. My tattoo."

"Why?"

"Because it's perfect in every possible way," he said with conviction.

"You're a perfectionist, then?"

"Hardly!" Trevor laughed. "I live in a world of compromise, but I respect and admire perfection when I find it." He let his gaze linger on hers until she blushed a little. "Your turn. Quick. I have to go."

"Tristan, the raven. He makes me laugh."

"So, you value laughter over other things."

She considered that. "I think maybe I do."

"Not happiness?"

"Aren't they the same?"

"Linked but not the same. You can laugh even when you're not happy."

"Rueful laughter, though."

"Still laughter and still the best medicine." When she nodded thoughtful agreement, Trevor spun away. He served the rest of the bottle, checked on the supplies and opened a couple more bottles for the waiters. Then he raced back down the corridor to clean the last of the rooms with Jenny. They were becoming quite an efficient team, and he teased her about that as they finished the last one. The phone was ringing, so she hurried back to the front desk, and it turned out several guests had changed their mind about staying, after all. Trevor helped her get through the cancellations and check-outs, one eye on the weather outside the big glass windows.

"You live in town, right?" he asked her and she nodded. "Feel like serving dinners? Double pay, then you can go home once the dancing starts."

Jenny, Trevor knew, was going back to college in January and had asked for extra hours over the holidays. "I have a white shirt in my locker," she said. "But what about the front desk?"

"I'll manage it. It's a good place to keep an eye on things."

"Deal. I'll stay even later if you need me."

"Thanks, Jenny. Are you coming back to the lodge in the spring?"

"I hope so."

"Then I'll talk to Gabe about a managerial job for you. You're really helping out today, but then, you always do."

Her smile was brilliant. "Thank you, Trevor!"

"And if you ever want to leave Honey Hill, whatever property I'm managing has a place for you. There aren't nearly enough people with initiative in this world."

She paused to look at him. "Where are you going to go?"

"I don't know yet, but I'll let everyone here know where to find me."

"Thanks, Trevor!"

The lights flickered and Jenny froze, turning back to look at him. He had time to see the question in her expression before the power went out. "Candles," he said tersely, reaching for the coat and boots he kept in the office. "I'll start the generators for Spencer. He'll need every bit of power to get those dinners served hot."

"I'll build up the fires, too," Jenny said and darted into the restaurant. Trevor headed out back to start the generators.

What was he going to ask Chynna?

Did he dare to ask her what he really wanted to know?

Chynna was amazed. The dinner was beautifully presented and hot, despite the power being out. She didn't think she'd ever eaten a more delicious vegetarian holiday meal and the others at her table were similarly impressed by their dinners. The fires blazed in the restaurant and the room was cozy with candlelight. The blinds were closed against the sight of the falling snow and she felt as if they were all enclosed in a safe haven. People seemed to forget the storm, or at least be complacent about it since they'd already decided to stay the night. She caught glimpses of Trevor in a heavy coat and boots, and recognized the woman from the front desk serving tables.

He intrigued her and even though she knew he was trying to capture her interest, she had to admit that he was doing a brilliant job. She couldn't find fault with a man who thought one of Tristan's best tattoos was perfect, much less one who'd made his peace with compromise in an imperfect world. She couldn't argue with his conviction that love needed attention to survive and thrive, and his certainty that expectations shaped results made her reconsider about her own assumptions. He was clearly used to working hard and to doing things right, and she admired those traits, too.

And then there was the sex. Chynna knew she was looking forward to more of that.

After they cut the cake and distributed the cupcakes, Gabe and Lexi led the way back to the conference room, where the fairy lights were lit again. The DJ had hooked a pair of phones to the speakers and though the room was a bit chilly, Chynna knew it would warm up soon. Just as Gabe led Lexi toward the dance floor, Lexi's phone rang, echoing loudly in the room. She answered it, then smiled for the other guests when she ended the call. "Teresa, Brad and Kristen are safely in Portland," she told everyone and there was applause.

Then Etta James began to sing *At Last* and Lexi stepped into Gabe's embrace. They were so completely fixed on each other that tears rose to Chynna's eyes. This was a marriage that would survive. They'd taken so long to come together that she knew they'd defend what they'd found and it made her glad. The next song was *Just the Way You Are*, and other guests began to join them on the dance floor. Chynna felt a hand on the back of her waist and smiled as she turned to Trevor.

"Done for the day?" she asked, unable to hide her pleasure. "Mission accomplished?"

"Just a small break to sustain me," he said, gesturing to the dance floor. Chynna smiled and they began to dance.

"You're still calculating," she said, seeing how his gaze roved over the room.

"Two big generators, thirty occupied guest rooms, plus several staff rooms," he said. "Hot water heaters, furnaces and lights." He winced.

"Too much for two generators?" Chynna guessed.

Trevor nodded. "Way too much. Time for triage."

"Maybe everyone should just go to bed and snuggle."

"Maybe we could play some very romantic music and encourage that."

"Maybe some of us don't need that much encouragement."

He looked down at her and she knew she had his attention again. "I like the sound of that."

She leaned closer and asked her question. "You have a lot of ideas about romantic love."

"I've thought about it."

"Have you ever been in love?"

"Is that another question?"

"Yes."

He shook his head. "I've been in lust many times, but then expectations do shape results. I've never had time for a long-term relationship or, really, the interest in building one. I've been completely committed to work."

"Regrets?"

"No."

Chynna hadn't thought he'd say anything else, given his choice of tattoo. She nodded and he looked down at her.

"You're not surprised," he noted.

"I've seen your tattoo."

"Does that mean you know all my secrets now?" he teased.

"I know a few of them, although you can't expect to keep them secret if you get a full sleeve to express them. Maybe you wanted someone to know."

"Maybe I was waiting for the right person to see the truth." Trevor smiled when she didn't answer. "I'd like to know what you think you see."

Chynna noticed that he was being evasive, which she knew wasn't characteristic of him. "My room this time," she said. "As soon as you're done for the night."

The song came to an end and Trevor bent to touch his lips to her ear. Chynna shivered with anticipation. "Give me twenty minutes. I'll meet you at the mistletoe."

There was nothing like the proper motivation to wind up Trevor's day. He strode through the kitchen, ensuring that clean-up was almost done, and conferred with Gabe about the generators, checked in at the front desk, sent Jenny and the other kids home, then locked up.

Chynna was waiting under the mistletoe, her eyes shining.

"There's an invitation I can't resist," he said, then caught her close and kissed her. There was no hesitation in her response: in fact, she seemed more passionate than she'd been the night before. He wasn't sure he'd survive that.

She broke their kiss all too soon and caught his hand in hers, leading him to her room. The sound of the music from the conference room floated through the hotel and made him smile. She lit dozens of candles as he watched and soon the room was filled with welcoming golden light.

"You prepared for this," he said with surprise and she laughed.

"Of course. The best seductions are planned."

Trevor liked the sound of being seduced.

Chynna closed the blinds against the chill of the snowy night and kicked off her shoes. "Do you think there's still hot water? I'd love a shower."

"I'd love one, too, but I think we'll have to make do with a wash. You first."

"Always a gentleman," she said, then crossed the room, framed his face in her hands and kissed him.

He moaned with satisfaction and drew her closer.

This was what he'd needed all day long.

That she had initiated the kiss was awesome: that

she apparently couldn't wait was icing on the proverbial cake.

Trevor sank into Chynna's kiss, drawing her closer, noticing how she welcomed him more than she had the night before. She was more open and more passionate, perhaps more trusting, and he loved the change. Her fingers were in his hair and there was an urgency about her touch that was new.

And exciting.

She loosened his tie without breaking their kiss, pushed his jacket over his shoulders and unbuttoned his shirt. Her hands were on his chest, then unfastening his belt buckle. Trevor kicked off his shoes and scooped her up, carrying her to the bed. She laughed when they tumbled to the mattress together and he rolled her over to unzip her dress. It was a sleek little black dress with long sleeves, one that hugged her curves and flared at the hem. He'd admired it all day long. She tugged it over her head and flung it at a chair then smiled as she knelt before him, her hair tousled and her eyes shining. Trevor stared, surprised by her black lace lingerie. She was wearing sheer lace-topped stockings and a black lace teddy. With her tattoos in shades of gray and her pale hair, she looked like a black-and-white pin-up.

But she wasn't just a picture.

And she was with him.

"Surprised?" she asked.

"Yes and no. Impressed."

"I believe in dressing for success," she purred.

"You caught me off guard last night."

"No regrets?"

"Only that I wasn't prepared." She beckoned to him with that wicked smile, the one that made his pulse go crazy. "Come here and be seduced," she purred.

Trevor couldn't shed his clothes quickly enough. "I should shower," he protested as she ran her hand down his chest again.

"I like how you smell," she murmured and rose to her knees to kiss his nipple. "I like your cologne and I like the smell of your skin." She looked up at him through her lashes, a coy glance that made his heart thunder, then grazed his nipple with her teeth. "It makes me want to take a bite," she whispered.

Trevor caught his breath then speared his fingers into her hair and drew her close for a kiss. Chynna tasted like cupcakes and champagne, and he wanted more than a bite. Her perfume was sweet and musky, mingled with the scent of her skin and her arousal. Her hair was like silk in his hands and her skin was just as soft. He could feel the strength in her body, though—she was sleek and powerful— and her kiss was fabulously hungry. She hadn't even glanced at his tattoo: this was all for him. Trevor closed his eyes and surrendered, loving how she clutched his head and feasted upon his mouth, as if she couldn't get enough. He had the sense that she'd eat him alive and he didn't care. He was ready to be whatever she wanted, to give her whatever she wanted, and to do it for as long as possible.

She made a little sound of desire that sent fire through his blood as he ran his hands over her. She winked as she rolled him to his back, then straddled him, her heels digging into his upper arms as she bent and took him into her mouth. Trevor heard himself moan, then he opened his eyes and moaned again at his view. He caught her hips in his hands and drew her closer, opening the snaps at the crotch of her lingerie with his teeth. He eased aside the lace with his tongue then flicked his tongue against her slick heat. When his mouth closed over her, she gasped and shivered, then her knees clenched around him. Trevor didn't surrender and Chynna laughed a little before she began to torment him with her lips and her tongue.

This was heaven. He could feel the lace beneath his hands and see it over her skin. He could feel her becoming more excited, quivering with her desire, and knew that he was about to explode. She rocked over him, moving with the precision and power of a dancer, and Trevor knew he wouldn't last long. He didn't want to stop either, but coaxed her on, hearing her little moans of pleasure, feeling his own desire burn.

She flicked her tongue against him, making him moan, then reached for the nightstand. She smoothed the condom over him then turned around to face him, her eyes sparkling and her hair tousled.

"I want to ride you," she said, straddling him again. She held his gaze as she took him inside her and Trevor caught her breath. She was so tight, so slick, so sexy. "I want to wrap myself around you," she whispered. "I want to pump you dry."

"Yes," he whispered, almost overwhelmed.

She bent down and rubbed her breasts against him, letting him feel the lace. His hands were full of her buttocks and he slid his fingertips under the tops of her stockings. So hot. So tight. So sexy.

"You like lingerie," she whispered.

"I like you."

"And lingerie."

"And lace," he confessed. "You wearing lace. I didn't expect it."

She moved her hips and he rose against her, liking how her eyes widened at the size of him. "You like surprises?"

"Good ones."

Chynna laughed a little. She bent down and put her lips against his ear, her breath making him shiver. "I want you to stretch me wide, Trevor Graham," she said and he appreciated that she was letting him know that she knew exactly who she was with. That she was talking dirty to him was also enough to make him explode. "I want you to give me the best orgasm of my life. I want you to make me scream so that the other guests come knocking at the door." She flicked her tongue across his earlobe. "And in return I'll shake the foundations of your world."

She'd already done that, but Trevor wasn't going to tell her.

He was going to seize the moment and enjoy.

"Kiss me," he whispered in invitation, and felt her laughter before her mouth closed over his. He gripped her hips and she rode him, moving so slowly that he was sure she'd kill him. She kissed him all the while, languid open-mouth kisses that could have been designed to steal his soul. Trevor was completely enchanted, enthralled by her touch, and only hoped he could last long enough to see her satisfied.

If Chynna did kill him, this had to be the way to go.

She blew his mind.

Twice.

Once with her lingerie on and once after he took it off. The second time was against the wall in the bathroom, but Trevor still hadn't had enough. Chynna had some kind of magical touch: no matter how often he had her or in how many ways, he wanted more. He still wanted her as if he hadn't had her at all.

That was a seriously good portent for the future.

So was the way that she'd screamed in her release both times.

"They're going to come knocking at the door," she whispered afterward, blushing slightly.

"You're going to have a line of volunteers," Trevor replied.

She ran a fingertip down his chest. "I only need the one I already have."

He caught her close and kissed her again, liking

that she clutched at his hair. He carried her to the bed and spread her legs wide, holding her captive to his touch as he went down on her again. She came quickly and roared with satisfaction, then they laughed together as they lounged on the bed.

"Give me a minute," Trevor said, tucking her into that plush robe. She curled up beside him, looking as contented as a cat. He wanted the night to last forever. "When exactly are you going back to the city?" he asked, not because he wanted her to go, but because he wanted to know how much time they had left.

"Tomorrow afternoon." Chynna looked at the clock but the display had gone out with the power. "Maybe it's today. I have a train booked from Portland after lunch."

"So you'll be back in Manhattan for Christmas."

She nodded and winced.

"Plans?" he asked and she shook her head.

"I always spend the 25th alone."

"No raven?"

She smiled, to his relief, but didn't meet his gaze. "Alone with Tristan the bird."

"No friends?"

"Too many memories. It's a hard day for me and I don't want to inflict that on anyone."

"Why?" Trevor asked, but he was pretty sure he could guess.

"Tristan died on Christmas Day." She reached out and traced the two koi on his arm with her fingertips and he saw her expression soften.

"Nothing like a shit anniversary to spoil the fun," he said. "I'm sorry."

"Thanks." She looked up at him. "You have one, too?"

He held up two fingers and she studied him for a moment, but didn't ask. He was glad.

Chynna's gaze dropped to the tattoo again and her own restless fingers. "Twelve years ago, you said." Trevor nodded. "No wonder it's so good. He was at the top of his game then." Her finger slid over his skin. "This might have been one of his last works."

He could have felt that three was a crowd, but he knew she needed to talk about Tristan. "Tell me about him."

Her gaze flicked to his. "Does that count as your next question?"

"I don't know. Does it?"

She frowned. "We should make a trade to keep in the spirit of your game. It should count."

"Okay," Trevor agreed, wondering what she'd suggest.

"I'll tell you about Tristan if you tell me about yourself first."

"Me? What about me?"

Her eyes narrowed as she studied him, giving her a purposeful look. "I don't believe you've never been in love."

"You should. It's true."

"Then you've chosen not to be in love," she said, her tone a little harder. She sat up and he missed her touch. "And I want to know why."

Ah. Trevor averted his gaze. "You could read my secrets from my tattoo instead."

"I could name some of them," she said to his surprise. She traced the outline of the lotus blossoms, then the second koi again. "No one gets to our age without falling in love at least once. Tell me about the one who got away."

"She didn't get away. I let her go." Trevor was surprised to have admitted as much, but once it was said, he couldn't take it back. "It was better for her that way."

Chynna smiled. "You must know that noble heroes are sexy." She walked her fingertips up his arm, and her tone turned thoughtful. "Although I'm not surprised."

"Can you be surprised?"

"Of course." She tapped his arm. "But a koi tattoo like this has several meanings."

"Tell me," he invited, glad of the distraction even though he knew the meaning of his ink.

She outlined the fish swimming up his arm. "Koi are symbols of overcoming adversity and transformation."

"Because they swim upstream."

"More than that." Her fingertip ran up and down the length of his tattoo, tracing the outline of one fish and then the other. "Do you know the story?"

"I'm not sure."

"Once upon a time, an enormous school of koi

swam up the Yellow River in China, until they reached a waterfall. There were thousands of fish but most of them turned back after several attempts to jump the falls. Some of them stayed, continuing to try to leap over the falls. These koi were so persistent that they kept trying over and over again, undaunted by their failure. After a hundred years, one of them finally managed to leap over the falls and the gods were so impressed that they turned this koi into a golden dragon. The falls were named the Dragon's Gate and it's said that any koi that manages to make it over the falls will become a dragon."

"I'm going to guess that not many of them do."

"Why?"

"Not many dragons in the world." It was meant to be a joke but Chynna didn't smile.

"Just because you don't see them on every corner doesn't mean they don't exist. I thought you would be one to look beyond the surface."

"I am, but I don't go looking for dragons."

She shrugged, letting that go. "This koi swimming up your arm is about facing adversity and seeking success despite the odds. It means there are obstacles before you, or there were when you chose the tattoo, but that you're gaining strength from the fight. It's a blue and black koi as a tribute to your masculinity and ambition, your independence and your resolve. It means you're driven to achieve your goals and is an expression of hope in your own strength. The color black is also indicative of success, either hoped for or attained."

Trevor nodded. He'd known all that when he chose it.

"You researched it, didn't you?"

"It's not something I wanted to fuck up."

She traced the other koi, her fingertip sliding over his skin. "This one refers either to achieving your goals or surrendering them in defeat. I'm going to guess that it means the first option."

"You'd be right."

"And it's gold because you associate success with financial security. A *yamabuki* like this means fortune and wealth. Was it a hope or an achievement?"

"It was starting to happen when I got the tattoo, but now I'd say my goal is achieved."

"And there are lotus flowers floating around the koi, symbolizing transformation. The lotus starts to grow on the river bottom, in the mud, but then stretches toward the light and blooms in beauty. It usually means that there are ongoing challenges, but that the bearer intends to overcome them."

Trevor nodded. "You're good at this."

"I had a good teacher. Do you overcome challenges?"

"I try to. The way I see it, you've got to keep moving forward. You've got to keep learning, and you've got to listen to other people."

"But if you're always moving, how do you put down roots?"

"Maybe I don't need roots. Maybe that's not for

everybody." It sounded like an excuse even to Trevor's ears and he sensed that Chynna didn't agree with him.

She pursed her lips and considered his tattoo again. "You have two koi, swimming in opposite directions, symbolizing balance and harmony. I'm going to guess that for you that's the balance between ambition and achievement." She met his gaze, surprising him a little. "But when is enough enough? How much will you surrender for your ambition? What will you surrender for it?"

Trevor was startled. He didn't think he'd given up anything.

Then he thought about being successful but alone.

Chynna dropped her gaze to watch her fingertip again. He thought she might surrender the topic, but she suddenly frowned and looked up at him. "What did you surrender, Trevor? And what did you have to overcome? That's my next question."

It was his instinct to refuse to answer. His reply would reveal a past he never discussed, but then, wasn't that the same confession he wanted from Chynna?

"That's two questions."

"You don't have to answer either of them." She waited and watched and he knew that answering was the price of hearing about Tristan. Not long ago, he would have walked away from a woman who made even this much of a demand, but Trevor didn't want to leave. It wasn't just that the room was cozy or that the sex was great. It was Chynna. She intrigued him.

He wanted to know more about her, too.

He wanted to know everything. He wanted to unravel her ability to fascinate him. He wanted to be with her, and for more than a night or two. It only made sense that there was a concession he had to make. Everything had a price, especially anything worth having.

Trevor chose to pay hers.

"Free pass," he said, his voice husky. "This story for your story of Tristan." He offered his hand and Chynna slipped her hand into his without hesitation.

"Deal," she said, then smiled. "But you first."

Trevor leaned back on the bed and Chynna watched him choose his starting point. She'd thought he would refuse to answer her and was already honored by his trust. She liked how direct he was and admired that he was decisive. It was fascinating to watch his eyes as he weighed the pros and cons, just a flicker in their depths while he calculated and then chose. She doubted that he ever had regrets. He was like Tristan in that, and maybe had something to teach her about savoring the moment.

Was it a lost love that drove his ambition? Was he rootless because he couldn't have the home base that he wanted? Chynna was curious, more curious than she knew she should be about a casual partner.

Funny how she didn't mind being drawn in by Trevor. He wasn't a man who would ever cling to a woman or a relationship. He didn't need help and he didn't need pampering. She would imagine that he would be an equal partner in every way, unafraid to pull his weight—no matter what needed to be done—and ready to step up for someone he loved. He was devoid of gender role expectations—she'd noticed that he'd cleaned rooms that day—and she liked that. He observed, assessed and chose.

"I grew up in foster care," he confessed, to her surprise, but then she realized that might explain his self-sufficiency. "My parents were killed in an accident when I was four, and I don't remember them very much. We didn't have any other relations, or none willing to take us on, and there wasn't much money, so into foster care we went."

"We?"

"I have a younger sister. She wasn't even a year old when it happened." Regret touched his expression and Chynna knew that sister had been important to him.

"What's her name?"

"It was Joanna."

"Was?"

"She was adopted, pretty much right away, and they changed her name." He cast his gaze downward and Chynna knew it wasn't a coincidence. He was hiding his thoughts. "They took her away," he said softly and she felt the ache of his sadness, even after all these years.

"Not you?"

"They only wanted a baby."

"Weren't you adopted later?"

"No. I was never adopted."

Maybe that was why he averted his gaze. That rejection must have hurt.

"New Year's Eve. One of those shit anniversaries I never forget."

Chynna understood that well enough. One was plenty for her. "Mine's Christmas Day," she confessed and he took her hand.

His smile was sad. "You always work the holidays, too?"

"I volunteer at a soup kitchen every year."

"That's nice." He squeezed her hand. "I just work. It's a welcome habit in this business and it's better to be busy than to sit alone and think."

Chynna nodded.

Trevor frowned and continued, still holding on to her hand. "I moved from one foster home to another until I could legally leave. On my eighteenth birthday, I was out the door with all my worldly possessions. I didn't even say goodbye."

"No lasting ties?"

Trevor shrugged. "Some of them were good people and some were less so. Some were well-intentioned, and others less so. I wasn't a very good kid and that certainly influenced results. In hindsight, I could say that I felt ignored if not forgotten, so I drew attention to myself in the only way I knew how. I got into trouble. Over and over again. Not big trouble. I don't have a juvenile record. But I challenged expectations. Every time I moved to a new foster home and had a new opportunity, I found the same kind of trouble again. I had a social worker tell me I had a homing instinct for it, but the truth was that I went looking for it. It was a habit. There were always kids who had no interest in getting good grades or excelling in school, always ones who stole or vandalized other people's stuff, and I always found them. Petty stuff, nothing serious enough to be charged, just really indifference to any path that would help me to achieve anything in life. I was lazy and unreliable, maybe a little bit charming."

Chynna smiled as he fell silent. "Maybe more than a little bit."

"Mad at the world maybe. I was sure it was unfair."

"That's not crazy, given your experience."

"But it wasn't constructive either. I learned enough to get by but had no interest in achieving anything or building anything."

"I'll guess that changed."

Trevor nodded. "I didn't have a plan when I left. I was just going to be independent. Free." He smiled and shook his head. "The thing was that I had no money and it wasn't that easy to get a job when I hadn't had one before. I ended up on the streets. I was hungry. I was afraid. I was going through the garbage at a diner by the docks early one morning when the owner caught me. He literally caught me. I tried to run but he grabbed me and shoved me into the diner. I was really afraid when he locked the door behind us. He was a big guy. But he heated up the grill and made me breakfast. I thought it was a trick, but it was hot and it was good and I practically licked the plate clean. Then he offered me a job."

Chynna smiled.

"What?"

"You'll see when it's my turn. Go on."

"He said the job would kill me or cure me, and I didn't know what he meant. He also said it was time for me to learn what I could do. I was glad of the chance, glad enough to follow his rules instead of breaking them. Being homeless had given me the motivation to grab at this chance. Bill let me eat as much as I wanted before opening and after closing, and I was able to sleep in the back room. I took out the trash and cleaned up the kitchen and cleaned the diner, too. I worked harder than I'd ever worked in my life and then he told me to work some more. I halfway think he lost money on that deal because I ate so much."

"Teenage boys can be impressive."

"I must have had three hollow legs." He shook his head, and she was glad that he smiled in reminiscence. "I was there about a year when Bill started to ask me for suggestions. No one had ever asked my opinion before, but I gave it to him. The place was busy sometimes but not consistently. I thought it looked grubby and told him so. I ended up getting the job of repainting the walls. I thought he needed more sandwiches on the menu, things people could easily take with them. I thought his fries weren't crispy enough and we talked about why. I thought he could offer a daily special or a coupon, something to mix things up. He didn't just discard my suggestions and I didn't make dumb ones. I thought about them and he listened. That encouraged me to come up with more ideas."

"He encouraged you."

"He listened. I learned that from Bill. You can't know everything. Other people aren't always right, but you can listen and you can decide whether they make sense or not."

"Sounds like a good strategy."

"We started working together, talking about changes and improvements, and damned if we didn't build the most successful diner in town. We had lines outside on weekends, then we had them during the week. We hired waitresses. We sourced pies from a local bakery. We stayed open later and we worked our asses off—and for the first time, I saw that I could make a difference if I wanted to. I was proud of what I was doing, and that was new. Bill was pleased because the diner was more profitable." He grinned. "We went shopping for new clothes and boots together. What a sight we were."

He fell silent again and his smile faded. His eyes seemed darker and Chynna knew he was reliving something painful. She waited for a moment before prompting him. "And then?"

"And then Bill died." Trevor swallowed. "He

just dropped one night while he was scrubbing down the grill. He died of a massive coronary right there in the diner. One minute he was telling me to add something to the wholesale order and the next he was gone. It shocked the hell out of me. Even though my parents had died, I never actually saw it. They left and didn't come back. This." He shook his head. "This was completely different."

"The paramedics couldn't help him?"

"They said it was instant." He frowned. "But he would have wanted it that way. The diner was his life. He'd been a cook in the merchant marine and cooking was what he knew. He'd bought the diner with his savings and it was everything to him. I remember these old guys would come in and spend all day there, just talking to him about old times as he cooked. Sailors passing through would stop to chat when they were in port. He poured them coffee and usually gave them a free meal. He was a good man and I missed him."

"The father you never had?"

"Something like that. He was gruff and didn't talk a lot. He could be kind, like he was to me and his old pals. He could be tough. He wasn't affectionate, but his heart was good. People trusted him. He taught me a lot, saved me, really, and I always wanted to be a credit to his memory. I had job offers right away, which amazed me, just because I'd worked with Bill and everyone knew it. What amazed me more was that he'd left me the diner. Lock, stock and barrel as he would have said."

"Wow."

"Yes. Wow. And there was a note that he'd written only a month or two before, telling me that I could do anything I wanted if I put my mind to it and not to become a lazy bum again."

Chynna laughed. "I'll bet you didn't."

"No way. I knew to listen when Bill spoke. I took the chance he'd given me and I ran with it. I promoted the cook who had been working part-time with Bill and went upmarket. He'd never thought that could be his style, but I knew I could make it work. New menu, new decor, but still appealing to the regulars. New pricing with some new ingredients. The place got trendy and revenue went through the roof. When it got to the point that there was a line every day for every meal, I sold it to the highest bidder."

"That must have been hard."

"It was, but I didn't think that kind of success could last. I thought I owed it to Bill to make the most of the opportunity he'd given me and I did. I moved to Bangor then, bought a failing restaurant in a great location, and did it all over again. Rinse and repeat for another eighteen years or so, Boston, Bangor, Portland and places in between, and here we are."

"But that's work," Chynna said. "What about love?"

"I love my work."

She shook a finger at him, choosing to tease him.

"You're ducking the question."

He didn't smile. "I was putting you on," he insisted but Chynna didn't believe him. "There never was a woman who got away. I never took the time to love anyone. I was working too hard."

"I don't believe you."

"You should." His tone was stubborn.

How strange that this very forthright man would suddenly become evasive.

Chynna knew it was important. He'd nudged her toward healing and she would nudge him back.

If Trevor wasn't prepared to really share—to play the game he'd started, by his own rules—then she wasn't going to talk any more to him about Tristan.

It was only fair.

CHAPTER SIX

Chynna rolled to her back and stared at the ceiling, choosing her words. She felt rather than saw Trevor lean closer. Was it a good sign that he was concerned by her reaction? He said he wanted more, but if he was going to keep his secrets, then his actions and his words didn't align.

Chynna wasn't good with that. She realized that she wanted far more than a single night, even two nights. She wanted more than pleasure and satisfaction. She wanted more than physical intimacy—she wanted emotional intimacy, and she wanted it with Trevor.

She'd take a lesson from him and admit it.

"What?" Trevor asked.

"Building restaurants to their potential is your passion."

"Pretty much. I think I'm good at it. It doesn't

leave a lot of time for anything else, but that's been okay to date."

"And you always sell the business when it's at the peak of its popularity."

Trevor nodded. "That's when its value is highest. It only makes sense."

Chynna rolled over to her stomach and looked him in the eye. "But if you can't commit to one restaurant, to sticking with it through the good and the bad, how do you imagine you'll be able to commit to one relationship?"

Trevor blinked. "You're not really talking about restaurants," he said softly and Chynna smiled. He frowned and looked across the room, then at her again. "But restaurants come into style and go out of it. There's a natural cycle to the business..."

"Does there have to be? Can't a business be built to a sustainable level, satisfying existing customers yet bringing in new ones at a steady rate?"

"There's always going to be some fluctuation."

She arched a brow. "Don't you think there's fluctuation in relationships, too? Times when things are awesome and times when they aren't?"

"Probably. That's why you need to put energy into a relationship to make it work over the long term."

"But that philosophy doesn't work for restaurants?"

She watched him think about that. She'd shaken his assumptions and she knew it. She was curious to see what he'd say next.

"It works for tattoo shops," she said. "You have to pay attention to sustaining the business as well as building it, attracting new customers and taking care of the ones you already have. Businesses are like relationships. They're not just an asset you buy and ultimately sell, or something that sits on the shelf and maintains its value. They have to be nurtured to grow and thrive."

"I guess a restaurant could be managed the same way," he said finally. "It would require a different marketing strategy, and a different menu. Less trendy. More consistent, but with a regular rate of change. I'm not sure how well it would work, though."

Chynna smiled. "You're only going to find out I'm right if you commit to something for the long term."

"Why does that sound ominous?"

"I think you're always on the move. I think you're always looking for the next thing instead of taking care of what you have, and I think that means that you'll always be shopping instead of investing. Restaurants or people."

"Go on," he encouraged.

"You're not insulted."

"I'm curious. I've never thought about it this way."

Chynna took a breath and confessed the rest of her conclusions. "I think that means that you're looking for a partner, but it might be more of a shopping trip. Even if that isn't your plan now, it'll end up that way because you haven't cultivated the skills to nurture anything for the long term." Sure she'd said enough and that he'd leave, she got out of bed and headed for the washroom.

"That's not unfair," he acknowledged to her surprise. "Don't you think people can change? Or that their goals can change?"

"Sure, but just because their goals change doesn't mean that their habits do."

"What would it take to change your mind?" Trevor asked and she turned to look back at him. He lounged on the bed, nude and gloriously male, his gaze locked on her. He had an ability to make her feel both special and very feminine. It was the intensity of his attention.

He listened and he was prepared to change his own thinking based on what he heard. She knew that was rare.

But she was realistic, too. "I don't think you'll do it. A desire to change doesn't always ensure change."

"Or else the world wouldn't be full of new diet plans," he said and swung from the bed to follow her. "You should give me a chance." His expression turned stubborn as he halted in front of her, that persistence coming to the fore. He braced his hands on his hips. "If you're going to issue a challenge, say it all, then see what I do."

"You might do it just to prove me wrong."

"You'll have to take that chance." He strode past her, moving with that athletic grace that made

Chynna's mouth go dry. Why were they talking instead of making love again?

Because this was important.

"Okay." Chynna folded her arms across her chest and watched Trevor as she challenged him. "Call your sister and wish her a merry Christmas. Reach out and reconnect with your past, then I'll believe that you can stick with something."

Trevor's shock couldn't have been more clear. His jaw nearly bounced off the floor. Chynna shook her head and went into the washroom, knowing she shouldn't be disappointed.

She certainly wasn't surprised that he came after her. He *was* persistent. "I can't do that," he argued.

"How did I know you'd say that?" She started to brush her teeth.

Trevor looked really agitated for the first time since she'd known him. He pushed his hand through his hair. "I can't intrude in her life. Not after all this time."

"Maybe she'd be glad to hear from you."

"Why would she?" He flung out his hands.

She really had hit a nerve.

"Because you're her big brother." Chynna kept her voice calm. "She was a baby. She can't remember anything bad about you."

"She can't remember anything good about me either."

"You might be surprised. She might have questions about your family. She might be glad to get in touch."

"She might be freaked out." He paced the bathroom, which was generously-proportioned but not that big. "It would be creepy. Like a stalker."

"It would be festive. Lots of people reconnect at Christmas." Chynna shook her head. "It's not like you're sending her pictures you took through her bathroom window when she wasn't aware of you being there."

"Still." He ran a hand over his head, swore softly, and paced some more. "I can't."

"Why not?"

He turned a blazing gaze upon her. "I just can't."

Chynna watched him, wondering. "It's kind of interesting that you haven't argued that you don't know where she is, or what her name is."

He shot her a look but didn't say anything.

"You *do* know where she is," she guessed.

"No. Not really."

"But you think you could find out."

"I don't know. Maybe."

"How?"

"You don't demand too much, do you?" That hint of a smile was back and Chynna was relieved.

"You want my biggest story. It's got to be a fair trade."

Trevor sighed and perched on the counter. "Okay. A few years ago, I had a bad feeling. I can't explain it. I just wanted to know that she was okay. I *needed* to know. When I have a feeling like that, I don't let it go."

"I would never have thought you were intuitive or psychic."

"Oh, I follow my gut all the time." He smiled down at her. "Why do you think I introduced myself to you?"

Chynna was startled. "Why?"

His gaze roved over her and his voice dropped low, making her shiver. "I just knew. I just knew I had to meet you and that there could be something potent between us. I had to know for sure." He held her gaze for a charged moment, then caught his breath and looked away. "Maybe I knew you'd shake my tree and that it might be good for me."

"Is this good for you?"

"I don't know." Trevor frowned, then shook his head. "Anyway, I made a lot of calls and found a lot of dead ends, but ultimately I talked to the social worker who had been in charge of our case."

"The value of persistence?" Chynna teased but he didn't smile.

"Something like that. She's retired now but she remembered us. I think she was glad to talk to someone, even me. She said her husband had died and she was alone. She said my sister was fine but that she couldn't give me any contact information. Joanna's married and her name was changed when she was adopted, and they have kids." He shrugged. "That's all I know. I guess it was supposed to be enough."

"Was it?"

"Yes and no. It was more than I was supposed

to know. I'm glad she's okay. Joanna was a baby when I last saw her, though. It's not like we were close."

"You should call the social worker back and ask to be put in touch with her," Chynna said.

"No." Trevor was adamant.

"Why not?"

"She might not want to hear from me."

"Then she can say so."

He was staring at the floor. "She can hunt me down if she wants."

"Why don't you want to pursue this?"

"I let her down." He gave Chynna a hot glance. "It was my responsibility to take care of her. It's the one thing I remember being told by our parents. But I didn't. They took her away."

"You couldn't take care of her," Chynna corrected. "You were only four."

He tapped the counter with a heavy finger. "I had a job to do and I didn't do it. I let her down."

Oh, he was principled and Chynna loved that.

"Why would she want to talk to me?"

"Because you're her big brother. You must be her only blood relation."

"She has kids now."

"It's not the same." She moved to stand in front of him, compelling him to look at her when he didn't reply. "You need to have permanence in your life of some kind, Trevor, even if it's a sister you call once a year. It's not natural to be rootless."

"And it undermines any argument I might make

about commitment in any other part of my life."

"There is that."

The corner of his mouth lifted as he held her gaze. "I thought I was the persistent one."

"Nobody said you had an exclusive."

He exhaled and looked around the room, but she knew he wasn't seeing any of it. She'd shaken him up but she hoped he was considering her suggestion. Chynna felt as if everything hung in the balance and she couldn't take a breath, wondering what he'd say or do.

She realized that she really didn't want Trevor to walk out of her life.

Not yet.

Then his phone rang and he darted across the room to retrieve it from his suit jacket. "Trevor Graham," he said when he answered, not looking at Chynna. He frowned as he moved toward the window and she wondered if it was bad news.

Why was Spencer calling him at this hour?

That was Trevor's first thought, but then he realized it wasn't that late. He could still hear the distant sound of music and laughter from the wedding reception. He went to the window to improve the reception and peered through the drapes.

All he could see was white.

"Hey, Trevor," Spencer said. "I just got home."

"Is the power out there, too?"

"No. We passed the crew on the road to the

lodge. A big tree came down and took out the power lines. I stopped to talk to them, and told them we had a lot of guests tonight. They said the power should be back on within the hour."

"Good. Thanks for letting me know."

"But the snow, Trevor." Spencer exhaled. "It's coming down like you wouldn't believe."

Trevor understood the implication. "Most of the guests were planning to leave tomorrow morning, but they might have to stay longer."

"I'm thinking so. It doesn't look like they'll have a choice."

"How are our supplies?"

"There's plenty for the brunch tomorrow, because I ordered extra anyway."

"The fridges and freezer are on, thanks to the generators, so there shouldn't be any spoilage."

"Right. When the electricity comes back on, could you check the fridges? The oldest one has a fussy compressor and you'll need to keep an eye on it. Sometimes it doesn't reset after a power outage."

"No problem. Tell me what to do." Trevor made notes as Spencer gave him instructions, then reviewed them with him to double check.

"I can do an inventory after brunch tomorrow and make a plan."

Trevor nodded agreement. "We'll have a better idea then how many will be staying."

"And maybe for how long. I'll put the plow on my truck now so I can get there in the morning. I should have done it already but it trashes my gas mileage." Spencer sounded rueful.

"I don't envy you that job tonight."

"Yeah, well, it's my own fault." Spencer cleared his throat. "Hey, everything was flawless today, Trevor. Gabe didn't even need to think about details and Lexi was so happy. Thanks for that."

"Just doing what I do."

"I'm going to talk to Gabe about closing the lodge for a couple of weeks, once all the guests go home. It's always slow in early January and I don't think we have any bookings this year. Sounds like a good opportunity for everyone to take a break."

Trevor's heart sank. He was going to be unemployed sooner than he'd expected. "Makes sense to me," he said with false cheer.

"We'll pay you, Trevor," Spencer said. "Just as we agreed."

"I had no doubt, Spencer. Thanks. See you in the morning." He ended the call, looking down at his phone. Money wasn't the point. He'd have nothing to do, and he really didn't like having nothing to do on New Year's Eve.

It was too easy to think then. To remember.

He glanced up to find Chynna watching him. She'd pulled on that fluffy robe again and her expression was serious. "Anything wrong?"

"Yes and no. The electricity should be back on shortly, which is good, but the snow is really piling up. Spencer thinks some guests might be required to stay longer."

Chynna went immediately to the window and

opened the drapes.

White. It was all white.

Trevor could hear the wind whistling, too, a sound that made him shiver. He turned his back to the snow and got dressed quickly.

"What else?" Chynna asked.

"What makes you think there's something else?"

She smiled. "You're ducking the question. He said something at the end, something you didn't like."

"I don't have an opinion one way or the other. I was just surprised."

"By?"

Trevor sighed, seeing no reason to hide the truth. "He's going to suggest to Gabe that they close the lodge for a couple of weeks after the wedding guests leave."

"How long were you supposed to stay?"

"Until the 10th of January or so. He said they'd still pay me."

She took a step closer. "But it bothers you that you'll be out of work."

"I like to keep busy." He found his tie and knotted it quickly, avoiding her perceptive gaze.

It made no difference. She still guessed, and in a way he was glad.

"Especially on New Year's Eve."

He reached for his suit jacket. "There's nothing saying I won't be working then. We might be snowed in, still."

She was beside him then, meeting his gaze in the

mirror. "Call her," she whispered.

Trevor shook his head, then pivoted to listen. "Did you hear that?"

"No. What?"

"The boiler came on again." He reached out and touched the switch on a lamp. The light went on. "The power's back," he said briskly, already forming a To Do list in his mind. "I've got to go check on things." He grabbed the list that Spencer had dictated to him and turned to leave.

"You're running."

"I'm keeping my responsibilities," he said, correcting her, even though she was right.

And he left, without a backward glance.

Chynna didn't make a sound. She didn't follow him. She didn't follow him into the corridor. She certainly didn't call him.

Should he be glad that she let him go without a fight?

Should he be glad that she was asking tough questions?

Should he call Joanna? The idea worried Trevor, although the more he thought about it, the less he was sure that was the case. Chynna was right. Joanna was his sister. She might have questions.

Joanna also might not want to know him. She'd found a family and a husband and had kids of her own. She might blame him for them being separated, even though they'd just been kids.

He came to a halt as he recognized the truth.

He was afraid she'd reject him.

That single realization changed everything. Trevor had never let fear stop him before and he wasn't going to do it now.

There was only one way to find out how Joanna felt. All he had to do was figure out how to contact her and give her the chance to get in touch.

He'd contact the social worker.

But first, he'd make sure that fridge had restarted.

Chynna had her hot shower, alone. She charged her phone, just in case the power went out again, and doused the candles. She closed the drapes again, but she could still hear the wind. She sat in the big bed, feeling that something was missing and knew it was Trevor's company.

There was a danger sign that she could miss him so soon after meeting him. It had been great, all she'd wanted and more. It was the more part that troubled her. Just as Tristan had always said, she wore her heart on her sleeve. She couldn't stop herself from getting emotionally involved. There was no such thing as a simple hook-up for Chynna and she'd proven it to herself for once and for all.

She wanted to know whether he'd contact his sister, and she wanted to know what happened. She wanted to help him through his shit anniversary, just the way he'd helped her through the wedding.

And she wanted to tell him about Tristan.

The urge to talk about that was new and troubling. Chynna debated the merit of sharing the story with a virtual stranger, knowing it might help her heal. On the other hand, she didn't want to let that story lose its power, or Tristan to lose his influence in her life. She missed him and still wanted him close.

Healing might mean being completely alone.

Chynna had trouble getting to sleep and awakened too late to go for a swim. She wondered if Trevor'd had time for one or if he was still working.

What would he decide?

The wall of pure white outside her windows startled her a bit, but no doubt people who lived with this weather knew how to deal with it. She was skeptical of Trevor's suggestion that the guests might be compelled to stay longer. She packed her bag once she'd showered and dressed, but left it in the room while she went for breakfast. Reyna hadn't sent her a message yet so she wasn't sure what time they'd be leaving for Portland, but maybe Reyna would be in the restaurant.

She wished that she and Trevor had parted better, but what was done was done.

Maybe being given the impetus to move forward had been the point of her time with Trevor. He certainly never lingered over the past.

Chynna was anticipating another of Spencer's buffets but found chaos instead. Trevor was on the phone at the front desk, apparently on his own, and there was a line of guests who looked unhappy. He'd changed suits and wore a different tie. He looked a bit tired and she wondered if he'd been there all night. Snow swirled outside the entry to the lodge. Chynna didn't disturb Trevor, particularly since he didn't even glance up, and went to have breakfast. The restaurant was crowded and disorganized. There was nothing on the buffet but she could smell coffee.

There was a clatter from the kitchen, though. Gabe was there with Lexi when Chynna peeked in, and they were obviously trying to deal with a crisis.

"What's going on?" she asked.

"Spencer can't get through the snow, and neither can any of the staff who live in town," Gabe said, speaking quickly. "We have a lot of hungry guests and cooking isn't my strong suit."

The coffee maker hissed as it finished its cycle and Lexi took the insulated pitcher into the dining room to serve coffee. Gabe was slicing away at the cutting board, doing an impromptu *mise-en-place*. He'd diced onions and chopped potatoes, and was slicing oranges and tomatoes to garnish the plates. His cutting wasn't as precise as Spencer's but it was a start. The grill was on, but nothing was cooking yet.

Chynna could fix that. She grabbed an apron and put some bacon on the grill. She broke a dozen eggs into a bowl and whisked them with a bit of milk. It was all second nature after her time at the soup kitchen and she worked with easy efficiency. Spencer's kitchen was beautifully organized—each time she wanted something, she looked in the obvious place and there it was.

She heard Gabe sigh with relief as she took some of the onions. "I didn't know you could cook." he said.

"I do a bit. Mostly I cook at the soup kitchen these days."

"So, you're used to cooking for many."

"Absolutely. Are there more eggs? I should start some more bacon, too. And there must be a toaster and some bread."

"On it," Gabe said, apparently just needing direction.

Lexi came back and started another pot of coffee. Chynna loaded up four plates with potatoes, scrambled eggs and bacon. Gabe garnished them and Lexi carried them into the dining room with toast. Chynna cracked a dozen eggs and whipped them in the bowl, then poured them onto the grill. She had enough bacon for four more plates. She started more potatoes, working in batches so each breakfast would be hot. When Gabe hesitated beside her, she said "toast" and he put more bread in the toaster.

"Woo hoo!" Lexi said when the next four plates were ready. "Chynna to the rescue!"

"Thank you so much!" Gabe said. He was starting to anticipate her, cutting vegetables and fruit to keep her supplied as she cooked. He added more plates to the stack beside her, too.

"It's not as fancy as what Spencer does, but no one needs to leave hungry," Chynna said with a smile. Another pound of bacon hit the grill and started to sizzle.

"No one's leaving at all," Gabe said. "Hungry or not."

Chynna turned to look at him, fearing that Trevor had been right. "But I have a train to catch in Portland. I have to get there."

He shook his head. "Not today."

"But I have to get back to New York. Today."

"You won't be going anywhere today," Gabe said. "The snow is two feet deep and still falling."

Chynna frowned and turned the eggs before they burned. She found it hard to believe that weather couldn't be overcome. Didn't people want to get on with their lives? Didn't they have plans?

Lexi returned to make more toast. "Is there any raisin bread? Someone asked."

Gabe pointed with his knife then kept dicing. "Check the fridge. I have no idea."

The three of them worked together quite well once they found their rhythm, putting out four breakfast plates at consistent intervals. The din from the restaurant diminished as people ate.

"I have to be in New York before tomorrow," Chynna said finally. "I help at the soup kitchen on Christmas Day. They need everyone and I go every year."

"They're going to have to do without you this year," Gabe said, his tone pragmatic. "Even if the snow stops this minute and the plows come right away, no one is going to be driving to Portland anytime soon. It'll be too dangerous."

They turned as one to look at the snow still falling beyond the windows. It was coming down so fast and thick that Chynna couldn't even see the railing on the deck, even though she knew it was twenty feet from the window.

"And the snow isn't stopping this minute," she said quietly.

"Not even close. We'll be lucky to see the plow by the end of the day. Maybe you'll be able to go tomorrow."

Chynna's heart sank. She still had to get to Portland to catch the train, which meant tomorrow night would be the earliest that she could get back to New York. "Everyone will be staying here."

"And most will be less happy about that than you," Gabe noted. He gestured with his knife. "Tomatoes, oranges, onions diced and coffee brewing. What else?"

"How many more people need to eat?" Chynna asked and Gabe went to make a count.

Not back in New York for Christmas. The prospect made Chynna panic a little. She had a routine to get herself through the anniversary of Tristan's death, and it didn't include being snowed in at a lodge in Maine. It required her to be busy, to continue Tristan's legacy by working at the soup kitchen, a long walk and a solitary dinner with her pet raven. None of those activities would be possible this year.

Maybe she'd cook here. If Spencer couldn't get to the lodge and everyone was compelled to stay, someone had to cook and it would keep her busy. It would be kind of like the soup kitchen. She could still retreat to her room after Christmas dinner and spend the evening alone with her memories.

If not her raven. He probably wouldn't know the difference.

She'd call Theo and check in, maybe get to hear that familiar croak.

It was a compromise but the best one possible under the circumstances. Once breakfast was served, Chynna would call the soup kitchen then Theo. She'd change her train reservation, then check the fridge and make a meal plan for lunch. Maybe Spencer would manage to get to the lodge before then. Maybe not. She should be glad to have a task to keep herself busy.

She wouldn't have expectations of Trevor.

She just wouldn't.

At least the power was on.

Trevor could smell breakfast cooking, though he wasn't sure who had taken charge in the kitchen. He was just glad that someone had. His stomach growled at the smell of bacon, and he was glad to see guests calm down a bit when they had the chance to eat something. Being hungry never improved anyone's mood.

He'd convinced the last of them that departure was impossible when a truck pulled into the parking lot of the lodge, its headlights on. It parked right outside the door and three woman hurried into the lodge.

It was Liv, with Lexi's mom and her partner. They all wore heavy coats and boots and were covered with snow, just from running that short distance. The two older women brushed the snow off their coats with relief and rubbed their hands together.

"Is there coffee?" asked Lexi's mom with obvious interest.

"Breakfast is on," Trevor said. "Please go into the dining room."

"I never thought hot food could smell so good," said the arty one, leading the way.

"The power went out at their house," Liv explained. "And the generator wouldn't start. Spencer had to plow most of the road to get there, and the driveway, too. They were freezing cold. There wasn't even any firewood, because they use the house so seldom in the winter."

"I'd thought they were going to spend last night here."

Liv shrugged. "I guess they wanted to be at their own place."

"Bad choice."

She smiled, her gaze sliding to the entry. Spencer's truck was on the move as he plowed the parking lot. The snow was falling so quickly that Trevor knew it would be deep again within the hour, but it couldn't hurt to start removing it. "Who's cooking?"

"I don't know, but it smells good."

Liv came behind the desk and shed her coat. "We ate at the house before we left. Spencer never goes anywhere on an empty stomach."

Trevor smiled at that.

"How long have you been at it?" Liv asked.

"I don't know. I checked everything once the power came on, then found a line here."

"Did you sleep?"

"I'll do that tomorrow." Trevor softened his words with a chuckle, but Liv didn't smile.

Instead she stepped closer to the desk. "Show me what to do and go get something to eat."

Trevor wasn't going to argue with that suggestion. He saw Lexi place loaded plates before her mom and partner as he walked into the dining room. They both looked delighted and began to eat with enthusiasm as Lexi went to get the coffee carafe and pour refills.

"Anyone else?" Chynna came out of the kitchen, her cheeks flushed and her apron spattered. Instead of a reply, she was given a round of applause.

She'd been cooking? Of course, she worked at the soup kitchen.

The lodge was a little more upmarket but judging from the expressions of the patrons, she'd done a great job. She flicked a glance his way, and he gave her a thumbs up. She blushed and turned to take off her apron.

Lexi carried out four more plates from the kitchen and beckoned to Trevor. "I was going to bring yours to the front desk."

"Liv has taken over."

"Then come sit with us."

Us meant Gabe, Lexi, Chynna and himself. There was another invitation Trevor couldn't refuse. They sat down to steaming plates and hot coffee, and Gabe thanked Chynna for helping out. Trevor guessed it wasn't the first time.

"It wasn't as fancy as what Spencer would have done," Chynna protested. "Just diner eggs."

"But good ones," Trevor said, saluting her with a piece of toast. "They say hunger is the best sauce."

Chynna smiled.

"Looks like a satisfied crowd to me," Gabe said. "Thanks again, Chynna. You weren't supposed to come here to work."

"Well, that's not completely true," Lexi teased. "I was hoping she'd work on my tattoo today."

"Lexi!" Gabe protested, but Chynna didn't look surprised.

"I wondered when you'd ask," she said. "I think we could get the outline done now that Spencer's here to do lunch."

"Yay!" Lexi said, throwing up her hands.

They laughed together, then Gabe sobered. "This is a good opportunity to thank you, too, Trevor. You really went above and beyond yesterday."

"Hey, we both have the same view of making it right, whatever it takes."

"But with the power out and staff low..."

"It was just as it shook out." Trevor continued

before Gabe could protest more. "I'll get even with you and have you manage my wedding."

"You? Married?" Gabe laughed. "Only to your career."

Trevor was well aware that Chynna was watching and listening.

"Everyone needs a passion," he said mildly.

Gabe cleared his throat. "Which reminds me..." He put down his knife and fork and looked steadily at Trevor. "I was talking to Spencer this morning."

Trevor nodded, trying to make the inevitable confession easier. "He told me that he was going to suggest closing the lodge for a few weeks when the guests leave."

"I think it's a good idea. We don't have any reservations and staffing is a bit of an issue with this weather." Gabe frowned. "The only thing is that you'll be done a few weeks earlier than we'd planned."

"This whole gig has been about surprises," Trevor said, keeping his tone upbeat. "Maybe it's better this way."

"You can stay if you want."

Trevor shook his head. "Better to head out."

"We'll pay you to the end of January, of course, as planned..."

"Spencer said as much."

"I'm sorry it didn't work out, Trevor. I feel like I misled you."

Trevor smiled. "Who can predict the twists and turns of true love?" He offered his hand and met

Gabe's gaze. "I'm glad it worked out for you, Gabe. I can't regret that you and Lexi are so happy together. No hard feelings. And it was a smoothly managed wedding, if I say so myself."

"Everything was perfect," Lexi said. "Thank you, Trevor."

"Not the power failure," he noted, sparing a smile for Chynna. She was listening avidly even as she ate.

"But you rolled with it so well. Thanks."

Gabe persisted. "But you regret leaving the lodge?"

"I think you've got something really special here." Trevor grinned. "I'm officially jealous. You can take credit for refining my idea of what my next challenge should be."

Gabe smiled with relief and they shook on it, then he got to his feet. "Sit," he said when Trevor would have stood up, too. "Have your breakfast."

"There's a lot to do," Trevor protested.

"And I'll do my part now. What's the forecast on the storm and the roads?"

"I think most people will be able to drive out in the morning," Trevor said.

Gabe nodded. "Okay, we'll plan to shut down tomorrow. Okay?"

"Sounds good." Trevor watched as Gabe headed to the front desk. Lexi returned to the kitchen to make more coffee and he was aware that Chynna was still watching him.

"Are you disappointed?" she asked in that soft

sultry voice that got him right where he lived.

"Of course. But that's how it goes." He fixed her with a look. "From where I sit, I see two paths. I could be angry, even resentful, and take the view that I've been jacked around."

Chynna's words revealed that she'd guessed the direction of his thoughts. "But they didn't do it on purpose."

"No. Everyone was trying to do the right thing, and shit happened. How could I resent my friend being happy?" Trevor shook his head, not waiting for an answer. "Or, I can see it as a learning opportunity, a chance to try something a little different and have my horizons broadened. I've been remaking and flipping restaurants but now I can see the appeal of a broader challenge, like the lodge." He shook a finger at her. "You're part of that inspiration, too. I'm also wondering now what it takes to build a business that grows and sustains, instead of peaking and dropping."

"Glad I could help," she said with a smile and sipped her coffee. She put the cup down. "I thought I'd offended you this morning."

"You surprised me, but I kind of like that." He held her gaze, letting her see his admiration. "It's new, but I could get used to it."

"I thought you were running."

"I was retreating to reconsider."

Chynna laughed and Trevor smiled.

"I think you're onto something, but I have to figure out how to address it."

Under the Mistletoe

"You are going to call your sister?" She looked surprised and a little impressed, which worked for Trevor.

"I feel like you've issued a challenge and I want to succeed at it."

"A knight on a quest," she teased.

"Something like that. But this one is tricky. I can't just call Joanna. I don't actually have her number. I don't even know her name for sure. Even if I call the social worker, she probably won't be able to do anything over the holidays."

"The record offices will be closed for the holidays."

"Right." He drummed his fingers on the table. "But there has to be another way."

"Is there anyone else who knew you both?"

"No. It was too long ago, and she was just a baby." Trevor's words faded. "Wait a minute." He shook a finger at Chynna. "The babysitter."

"From that night?"

"Yes, she lived down the street. Jane. Jade. Janet. Janice. Something like that." He frowned as he tried to recall her name. "I can remember what she looked like. She had these amazing dimples. So cute."

"Did you have a crush on her?"

He grinned. "Maybe a little. She let me stay up later than I was supposed to. And she always made popcorn." He snapped his fingers. "Jayden! That's it."

"Kind of an unusual name."

"I just have to remember her surname."

"She might have changed it."

"No negative thinking here," he admonished. "I'm on a quest and determined to succeed."

Chynna laughed. "I like seeing persistence in action."

"You won't say that when I turn the tables on you."

"How so?" She didn't look very worried about it.

"It's time to reciprocate. I've celebrated my shit anniversary, so to speak, by working every holiday and pretty much avoiding any recollection of it. That didn't help me to put it behind me, even though I was pretty sure that was what I was doing."

Chynna nodded. "And I've celebrated my shit anniversary by working at the soup kitchen, spending time alone with my pet raven, and reliving my memories."

Trevor noticed again that they had common ground. "Has that helped you put things behind you?"

Chynna shook her head. "You know it hasn't."

"And I'm glad you admit it. So, what are you going to do differently this year?"

"Well, I won't be working in the soup kitchen tomorrow. I'll be on my way home."

Trevor gave her a look. "It doesn't sound like Tristan the raven is missing you that much. I mean, he's got someone keeping him in old movies and someplace to tap dance."

"True." She fought against her smile and lost. Her eyes even twinkled in anticipation of whatever he would say. "Go ahead, Trevor Graham. Challenge me. I'm due for a quest."

Trevor grinned and leaned closer, knowing he could get lost in her eyes. "I challenge you to mix it up. To do something different, instead of running back to New York."

"Like?"

"Take a road trip with me."

She sat back with surprise and he feared he'd asked too much. "What?"

CHAPTER SEVEN

Trevor knew he was talking fast. "I'm going to be unemployed tomorrow. What do you say I drive you back to New York, but we take our time and do some sightseeing on the way?"

"I don't know..."

"Whoever drives you to Portland tomorrow to catch your train will miss the party at Jane's, right?"

Chynna frowned. "I hadn't thought of that. Reyna will want to go."

"Of course. She's organizing it."

"But I should get back. I can take the train on Wednesday."

"You could. When was the last time you took a vacation?"

"I don't remember."

"Me neither. Let's do it together and help each other undermine our shit anniversaries."

She eyed him warily. "That sounds like the beginning of something serious. Or a diabolical plan to turn a fling into something more."

"It sounds like a movie, actually," Trevor admitted. "*Planes, Trains and Automobiles.*"

"No, it would be a romantic comedy that ends happily."

"That one kind of was."

She laughed. "You're right. It kind of was. And a Christmas movie."

Their gazes locked for a minute. "Think of it as a favor between friends."

She lifted a brow. "And then?"

"And then you go back to your life and I carry on with mine. After a mistletoe interval, of course." Trevor smiled as she laughed, knowing that he was hoping for more of a future between them than that. Incremental progress, though, was the best he could hope for.

Chynna's eyes sparkled and he knew she liked the idea better than she was letting on. "Is this a platonic adventure?"

"Rated G?" He sighed, letting his feelings show. "It could be," he conceded and she laughed again. "Although at least PG-13 would be better."

She was fighting that smile again, and losing the war, again. "Lady's choice."

"Exactly, but you have to know that I'm hoping otherwise." He leaned across the table and dropped his voice to a whisper. "There's something addictive about the sound of you letting loose. It's really hot.

I want to make that moment last forever."

Chynna blushed, but her eyes twinkled. "I'm not sure I could survive that."

"We should try. Purely for experimental reasons."

"Uh huh. I do like how you make that happen," she confessed softly and he was ready to do it again. "I think it's a tongue thing."

"That's only half the secret."

"And the other half?"

"I'll never tell."

"Whatever you do, it's really hot."

He caught his breath and lifted his hands. "And I'm yours for the taking."

Chynna turned her cup in its saucer as if weighing her options, then impaled him with a glance. He braced himself for whatever she might say. "I like that, you know."

Trevor blinked in surprise. "You like what?"

"That you're direct but not pushy. You let me know what you'd prefer but you leave it up to me. I know that if I asked you to stop or said no, you'd totally honor that."

"Of course."

Her slow smile heated him to his toes. "And I like that. A lot. Just saying."

He leaned across the table again. "And I like you, a lot, which means you get to make all the rules. Just saying."

"There's no way you've never been in love," she said lightly. "You're too good at this."

Trevor didn't know what to say so he kept his mouth shut.

Chynna, to his relief, leaned closer, her eyes glinting with intent. "My room tonight. You owe me a report on your quest. I want to be on top, and I'll tell you when you get to come."

"And you owe me a story," Trevor said, trying to hide his surprise over her delicious threat. "The deal was sharing the story of my shit anniversary for yours."

"Deal," Chynna said, agreeing more easily than he might have expected.

"And the road trip?"

"You're on."

Trevor laughed out loud. "Ha!"

Chynna laughed, too. "We should shake on it."

"Forget that," he said, then stood up and caught her around the waist. She leaned against him, smiling. "Some deals should be sealed with a kiss."

"You're right," she said, turning in his embrace. Her gaze dropped to his lips then rose to meet his gaze again. "You're so very right." And she kissed him with such enthusiasm that Trevor wondered how much she'd been holding back.

He was pretty sure he was going to find out.

Soon.

Although it wouldn't be soon enough.

Trevor was right. It was time to move forward.

Chynna was actually looking forward to it.

She was also looking forward to surprising

Trevor more than she had. She liked how his eyes flashed when she'd agreed to his suggestion, as if he hadn't expected that. And she could tell that he hadn't expected this kiss. Some of the guests hooted and whistled as she backed him into the wall and then there was a smattering of applause. It wasn't like her to make a public display of affection, but she was having fun.

She'd likely never see most of these people again. Who cared what they thought of her? She only cared about shaking Trevor's assumptions.

They broke their kiss when Spencer came into the restaurant and was greeted with a shout. He was wearing a heavy coat and tall boots and was covered in snow. "You don't even need me anymore," he protested, surveying the empty plates. There was more laughter at that. "Thanks Chynna," he added, leading a round of applause for her.

"You haven't seen the mess we made in your kitchen yet," she teased and Spencer laughed again. Trevor kept his arm around Chynna's waist and she saw Spencer notice that, but he didn't comment.

"Can I keep your attention for a minute, everyone?" Spencer smiled as everyone fell silent. "I have a bit of good news to share with all of you." He offered his hand to Liv, who had followed him to the doorway to the restaurant. She smiled, blushed, and crossed the floor to take his hand. He pulled her close to his side, his expression revealing his feelings to everyone in the room. "Olivia and I were married last week."

Chynna smiled as the guests expressed surprise.

"You knew," Trevor whispered and she nodded. She touched her left hand and he nodded. "I wondered about that." He kept holding onto her hand and she liked that just fine.

"What?!" Lexi cried in the meantime and leaped to her feet. "How could you not tell us?"

"How could you not invite us?" their mom said, putting down her coffee cup.

Spencer raised a hand. "We didn't want to steal any of the fanfare of Lexi's big day. Olivia wanted a quiet ceremony. We decided to just do it and tell you all here, today."

"No party?" Reyna teased and the couple laughed.

"Lexi had a party," Liv said.

Reyna pulled out her phone. "And you need one, too. Give me five minutes." She called someone, walking into the lobby as she spoke.

"We just wanted to share the news with you all," Spencer said. "Please enjoy your breakfasts." He might have retreated, but Lexi, her eyes filled with mischief, picked up a spoon and started to tap on the water glass on a nearby table. Chynna laughed and did the same. Soon the restaurant was filled with the sound of tinkling.

"Kiss, kiss, kiss!" Lexi called and others took up the call.

Spencer laughed.

Liv blushed a little more. Then she reached up to frame Spencer's face in her hands and kissed him.

He dipped her and the guests laughed as they applauded.

Reyna returned to the restaurant and whistled for silence. "The reception will be tomorrow at Jane's house. She's invited everyone who wants to come. She has a turkey and makes the best stuffing."

"All we need to do is get there," Kade said.

"I saw the plows out," Spencer said.

"And the forecast is that the snow will stop tonight," Trevor said. "We should be clear for the morning if anyone wants to head out then."

There was another cheer, then he squeezed Chynna's hand. "Duty calls?" she asked.

"Will you go tomorrow?"

Chynna nodded, knowing she wanted to share the joy of Spencer and Liv's union. "It sounds like it might be a lot like the soup kitchen. Busy with lots to do."

"But Christmas," Trevor said.

Chynna nodded and met his gaze. Christmas. She remembered the holiday being a joyous one, once. Could she and Trevor help each other find that magic again?

"What do you say we go to the party, then head out for our road trip on Wednesday?" she whispered to him.

"Sounds like a plan. And now, duty calls."

She kissed him again, but more quickly, and watched him stride away.

⁂

Under the Mistletoe

Could Trevor find Jayden?

He had to think that her unusual name might make it possible. He remembered her surname, out of the blue, which vastly increased his chances of success. When things quieted down at the front desk, he retreated to the office of the lodge and used a desktop computer. He searched on her name and immediately found a dozen women with the same name. A number of the results were Facebook profiles. He had no time for social media himself, but now he created an account and went to look at their profiles.

Four were on the east coast, although certainly she could have moved. It had been twenty years. She might have married and changed her name, too. Hell, she might have died, or she might not be on social media, which in some circles was almost the same thing. He searched profiles and looked through the pictures that were publicly visible and within half an hour, he'd identified the most likely candidate.

Jayden was twelve years older than him. Her profile displayed her birthday and her hometown. She lived in a suburb that couldn't be thirty miles from where he'd lived as a child. Of course, she'd grown up, but he'd remember that smile anywhere. And those dimples. Her kids looked like her and he smiled as he scrolled through the pictures of her family.

Thank goodness for trusting people who made their photographs public. Jayden's oldest was finished with college. She seemed to use the account to keep in touch with friends from high school, because there were other names in her list of friends that sounded familiar to Trevor, and pictures of houses and restaurants that rang a faint chord. Maybe that was why everything was public. She was looking for connections.

He found a post that she was organizing the high school reunion in his hometown and knew he was right.

Trevor completed his own profile, adding a picture and some details about himself, then sent Jayden a friend request and a message. Would she be online at Christmas? She'd posted something earlier in the morning, and he didn't know what to do. He sat and stared at the screen, waiting, then felt someone behind him.

It was Jenny.

"You made it."

"Yup. I guessed you'd probably need me when my dad said no one would be checking out today."

"That's awesome. Thanks, Jenny."

She leaned over his shoulder to look at the screen. "Old flame?" she asked, her tone teasing.

"Babysitter when I was a kid," Trevor confessed. "I thought she might remember something about my mom."

Jenny sobered. "Your mom died?"

Trevor nodded. "When I was a kid."

Jenny leaned down. "But you weren't friends with her already, right?" Trevor shook his head and she claimed the mouse, navigating to his own inbox. "See? You have two mailboxes. One for friends and one for people who aren't friends. The other mailbox. Some people don't check it very often. Some people don't even know it's there."

Great. "So, I shouldn't sit here and wait for her reply?"

Jenny shook her head. "She might never see it."

Trevor exhaled, hating that it hadn't been such a brilliant idea, after all.

"Or she might be really compulsive about it. It just depends why she's there and how much she knows about it."

"Thanks." Trevor started to log out, but then there was a chime. "My friend request was accepted," he read and Jenny laughed.

"Okay, she's on it. Have a good chat. I've got the desk."

A message appeared in Trevor's inbox and his smile broadened when he opened it. His name was typed in all caps with five exclamation marks after it and a shocked emoticon.

TREVOR GRAHAM!!!!!
YOU GREW UP!
=8-O

Jayden remembered him.

He hoped she knew Joanna, too.

Contrary to the weather reports, the snow kept falling.

Chynna finished the outline on Lexi's tattoo that

afternoon, while Reyna and Liv sat and chatted. They heard the story of Liv and Spencer's engagement and their wedding, and admired her ring. It was cozy and quiet, but Chynna would have enjoyed it more if she'd known when she'd get back to the city. The manager at the soup kitchen had told her not to worry about her absence—one of the newspapers had run an article about the holiday meal and they had more volunteers than they could use. She'd be missed, though. Chynna told herself to be glad of that, but she felt unsettled.

She was thinking about Trevor, and knew she was more interested in him than should have been the case. She'd miss him, even if they agreed to go their separate ways immediately. There was something about that little mysterious smile, his persistence, and the attention he paid to making love. She liked him, a lot, and knew she could get used to having him around. She was excited about taking a road trip with him, but a little bit worried about risking her heart.

She wasn't as tough as she'd once been.

On the other hand, she felt alive again and engaged. Wasn't that worth any potential price? And who was to say they wouldn't work it out?

Why couldn't she just take things at face value? She should enjoy her time with Trevor for the moment, then let it go when it was over.

How hard could she fall in a week?

Chynna feared it would be pretty hard. She was already slipping.

But she couldn't fight her sense that Trevor was too good to be true. He'd been quick to deny ever having been in love before but she'd seen his expression when she'd first teased him about it. He had been in love and something had gone wrong. He'd shared one story of his past, and she should respect his privacy on the other.

After all, it was just a fling.

He was at the front desk when she came down for dinner, frowning a little as he reviewed something on the computer there. Chynna's heart skipped a beat and Lexi must have noticed her reaction. She gave Chynna a teasing glance, then hurried Reyna and Liv into the restaurant, leaving Chynna to talk to Trevor alone.

"Hey." Trevor glanced up and smiled, making her feel warm all over. His eyes always seemed to get darker and his gaze more intense, as if he was completely fascinated by her. "Did you have a good day, despite the weather?"

"I finished the outline on Lexi's new tattoo. Any news on the weather?"

"They say it's stopping." They turned together to look at the swirling white outside the windows. "Soon."

"Soon," Chynna echoed, her skepticism obvious.

"There's over three feet of it."

"That's too bad. No one will be going to Jane's tomorrow."

"Oh, I think where there's a will, there's a way."

Chynna had the feeling he wasn't talking about

road conditions. She met his gaze and saw that she was right.

"And thank you," he added softly, his attention so locked on her that she couldn't look away.

"For what?"

"For encouraging me to reach out. I talked to Jayden." He winced. "Well, we messaged on Facebook until she gave me her phone number and I could call her. Maybe I'm old-fashioned but I like to hear a person's voice."

Chynna smiled. "Social media not your thing?"

He shook his head. "No. But in this situation, it was great. I found her and she knows Joanna. Funny thing is that Joanna contacted her the same way a few years ago. She's passed my information along, so the ball's in her court, so to speak." He took a deep breath. "It was nicer than I expected to talk to Jayden. She remembered more good things than I did and it made me smile. Thanks for pushing me to it."

"I hope you get to talk to your sister."

"Well, it's up to her."

"You're not going to worry about it?"

"I have a policy of only worrying about things I can control. Otherwise, I let it go." He opened his hand as if dropping something from it.

Chynna could take a lesson from that. "It's a good plan."

"But one that takes some work in practice." Once again, he hid his thoughts from her. "So, tomorrow is becoming kind of a pot luck, with anyone local bringing something to keep Jane from having too much work to do herself. You probably didn't know, but guests have been in and out of Spencer's kitchen this afternoon, making family favorites to take along. It'll be more crowded in the morning, so if you want to make something, you'll have to get in line."

"I love that idea."

"Liv suggested it. I think it's a good one." He frowned and cleared his throat. "And I was thinking of what you usually do on Christmas Day at the soup kitchen. So I asked Liv if there were people in Honey Hill who usually spend the holidays alone. She's asked them to come, too."

"What a great idea."

"Turns out that Jane herself is often alone, and there's a bookseller who doesn't have family. A couple of others." Trevor smiled and Chynna caught her breath. "So, in a way, it's a tribute to you, for bringing the bride and groom together, to community here in Honey Hill, and to how you like to make a difference on the holidays."

Chynna smiled despite the lump in her throat. She reached out to touch Trevor's shoulder, then ran her hand over his strength. She wasn't thinking of the tattoo on his skin there, but of the man beneath the suit.

"Thank you," she whispered. "I'm so glad I'll be here."

"Me, too."

She was thinking of claiming another kiss but the

phone rang at the front desk and Trevor winced. "Duty calls."

"But not for much longer."

He nodded once. "Meet me for dessert?"

Progress was made.

Trevor felt like a superhero for having convinced Chynna to take the road trip with him. He would make it awesome and was already planning where they could stop.

"Wolfe Lodge," he said. "How can I help you tonight?"

"Is that Trevor Graham?"

He straightened in surprise, knowing the voice was familiar but unable to place it. It had been a while. "Yes."

"Michael Callahan," the caller said, his tone warming. "How the hell are you?"

"Mike! It's great to hear from you." Trevor had partnered with Mike for his second restaurant and they had made a terrific team. They shared a vision and had been so in sync that they'd finished each other's sentences. After they'd sold that restaurant, Mike had gone to California, and partnered with his then-new wife in multiple ventures. Trevor had heard stories about Mike's success over the years but they hadn't crossed paths again.

"Wouldn't have guessed that, since I didn't have your cell phone number."

Trevor laughed. "It's been fifteen years."

"Well, I heard through the grapevine that you

were working for Gabe at Wolfe Lodge and took a chance. I didn't think you'd be delegated to answering the phone. Don't tell me you've lost your touch?"

"Not a chance. We've got a blizzard here, and are really short of staff. All the guests are friends and family here for the wedding, so it's worked out okay."

"A Christmas wedding? Anyone I know?"

"Gabe got married. That's partly why I'm here."

"Married. That's not the story I heard."

"Well, it changed. Gabe was going to leave Wolfe Lodge so I came to take over his role. Then love conquered all and he came back to the lodge. I stayed to fill in for the wedding and his honeymoon."

"So, you're not buying in?"

"No. Even though I'd love to." Trevor saw no harm in admitting the truth to Mike. "This place has got it all."

"How soon will you be out of work?" There was definite interest in Mike's tone and Trevor wondered at that.

"It was supposed to be in two weeks, but it looks like I'll be done tomorrow."

"Excellent news!"

"I'm going to guess that you didn't call to wish me happy holidays."

Mike laughed. "No, I didn't. I'm glad I took a chance and chased you down. I heard you were buying in to Wolfe Lodge."

"That was the plan a few months ago."

"I'm sorry it didn't work out for you, Trevor, but I have an offer for you."

"The proverbial offer I can't refuse?"

"Maybe. I've got my fingers crossed. What did you mean when you said Wolfe Lodge had everything?"

"It's the perfect challenge. Great facility. Ideal location. No local competition. Fabulous chef."

"Spencer Wolfe?"

"Yes."

"I've heard he's good."

"Better than good. He's going to be a draw in himself. Gabe has the spa thing nailed and there are opportunities for local growth."

"Golf course?"

"And ski runs. Cross country skiing. Tasting tours. Cooking classes. It can be built into a year-round destination."

"Conferences."

"Business retreats. It's not that far from Bangor or Portland but feels like it's off the edge of the known world." Trevor sighed. "It's going to be huge."

"And you wanted to be a part of it."

"Who wouldn't?"

"Guess where I am?" Mike invited.

Trevor looked at the area code on the caller identification but didn't recognize it. "No idea."

"I'm sitting in a restaurant that is part of a planned hotel complex and retreat on the island of

Maui. It's open to the beach and I can see the beach and the ocean from here. I can feel the breeze as I watch the birds go by and smell the flowers."

Trevor smiled, because Mike had always had a gift for hyperbole. "I get it. Tropical paradise."

"And then some," Mike agreed. "The chef, who is amazing, is preparing local fish and produce."

"And you're married to that awesome chef, right?"

Mike chuckled. "She's even better than when I met her. Honestly, she's doing her best work out here. It's an inspiring environment and a great area. The locals already come here when they want a great meal. I'm taking surfing lessons, and we go snorkeling on Sundays. Paradise has nothing on this place. It's amazing and it's going to get better."

"Who are you working for?"

"Me. I bought it, Trevor. Anna is making magic in the kitchen and we're working the spa angle. I'm planning the amenities including a nine-hole golf course on the property itself, and access to another eighteen at the adjacent golf club. This project is going to be huge, so huge that I need another partner on the team. I immediately thought of you."

Trevor sat down hard. "I'd love to see it."

It sounded like everything he wanted.

But on the other side of the world.

"I'll send you a ticket," Mike said, then chuckled. "But you'd better brace yourself. I think you're going to take one look and decide to stay."

It was the opportunity he'd always wanted, and it

had dropped into his lap. Trevor couldn't believe his luck. He and Mike exchanged numbers, and within moments of ending the call, the flight confirmation appeared in his email.

He was going to Hawaii on January 10th.

And if Mike was right, he might not ever come back. His future had arrived.

It was funny, though, that for the first time ever, Trevor hesitated over an opportunity. He knew it was a good one. He trusted Mike. But he wasn't so sure that he wanted to leave the east coast.

He could keep in touch with Joanna wherever he was.

But what about Chynna?

Trevor was pretty sure that leaving would mean the end of whatever was beginning between them. Absence didn't make the heart grow fonder, in his experience. Just the opposite in fact.

He was going to have to choose.

But probably Chynna would do it for him.

He refused to let this opportunity change anything. He hadn't signed anything. He hadn't agreed to anything. He was almost unemployed and now he had a trip planned to Hawaii in a couple of weeks.

He decided by the time he went to have dessert with Chynna that he just wouldn't mention it to her. It might not be relevant, and if it became so, he'd tell her then.

Why did that feel like a bad choice?

Chynna was a tigress that night.

Trevor was amazed and thrilled. They barely made it over the threshold of her room before she backed him into the wall and kissed him. They stumbled toward the bed, stripping off their clothes as they went, necking like teenagers as they fell onto the mattress. She was unrestrained and demanding and Trevor couldn't get enough.

He went down on her, determined to make her come. He made her wait for it, teasing her as she writhed beneath him, loving how she shouted his name as she came. She didn't give him a chance to gloat, though. She tackled him and straddled him, moving so slowly that it was excruciatingly sexy. She took him to the cusp of release, then eased off, making him moan with need.

All the while, she whispered to him, telling him what she wanted to do to him, threatening to make him wait all night, describing her favorite lingerie. It was exquisite torture and when Trevor finally came, he shouted with satisfaction.

The second time was just as fast and hot and fabulous.

The third time was slow and seductive.

She yawned when they washed up together, but Trevor teased her. "No crashing out on me now. You owe me a story."

"I know." Chynna nodded, then tugged on that robe. She stretched up to give him a kiss and they ended up entwined again. Then he scooped her up and carried her to the bed, tucking them both in beneath the duvet. He was dead on his feet, but she was serious and he wanted to hear the story. "I met Tristan when I was a runaway kid. I was fifteen and living on the streets, not doing very well at it."

Trevor snorted. "More in common," he said and she smiled.

"I told you that you'd see."

He nodded. "You couldn't go home?"

Her lips set. "I didn't want to." She gave him an intense look. "I would have died before I would have gone back to that hell."

"Want to talk about that?"

"No. It's over. It's done. He's dead and I've been back to spit on his grave. It doesn't matter anymore."

Trevor wondered but kept quiet. Chynna might have come honestly by her reluctance to trust a sexual partner. If that was her only legacy of a bad upbringing, that was more than fair.

"The first time I met Tristan was when he brought me food. He must have noticed me in the neighborhood, but I hadn't seen him. I had my corner for panhandling and my routine, and then one night, this guy brought me something to eat. It was take-out from a fast food place. I wouldn't have accepted it otherwise because I was expecting to be tricked and victimized by that point, especially by men. The food was still hot and recognizable. I knew he couldn't have messed with it, and I was so hungry. I barely glanced at him, but I thanked him, and he left. When he came back the second night, I had a better look. He was maybe twenty years older than me and looked tough. He had tattoos everywhere it seemed. He was big, too, a huge man."

Trevor nodded, remembering.

"And he radiated this energy." Chynna's tone was awed. "He was charismatic and his presence was compelling."

Trevor nodded, remembering that, too. Tristan had been larger than life.

Who was he kidding that he thought there was room in Chynna's heart for both Tristan and him? In that moment, he doubted the chance of their shared future.

But he had Hawaii as a consolation prize.

"It was mesmerizing to be near him and I saw that as dangerous," Chynna said. "He wore this battered leather jacket and jeans that were torn at one knee. His hair was long enough that he tied it back in a ponytail and he had a full beard." She looked down, watching her fingertip trace a circle on the linens. "But he had the kindest eyes I'd ever seen." She nodded. "I wasn't very nice but he didn't seem to care. He said he didn't want anything from me—I asked—that he just didn't want to watch me die. It was fall, October, and it was getting colder at night. I didn't believe him, but I took the food again."

Trevor waited.

"He came every night. After a couple of nights, he asked what I liked best and I told him. We talked about food a bit, and the next night, he brought me Chinese food. For the next week, he seemed to want to surprise me—every night, it was take-out from a different place. I'd never had Thai food before, but I loved it. Rice and beans from the South American place, even sushi. And each night, we talked a little bit more. He pointed out his shop to me—it was a tattoo shop, just down the block, one I'd noticed before because of the activity and the music—and told me I could knock on the door anytime, at any hour, if I needed help. I thought he was shitting me."

"And then you thought he wanted something else," Trevor guessed.

Chynna nodded. "But he never touched me. He told me that he had a daughter the same age as me but that he never saw her and that was when I started to trust him. I could see how much the situation hurt him and I guessed that he was helping me because he couldn't help her. When the first snow came, I went and knocked on the door of his shop. I wasn't sure what to expect and I halfway thought I was stepping into a trap, but I was cold. I'd never been so cold before. I felt dirty, too, and on some level, I knew that if I stayed on the street, then I wouldn't see the spring."

She shook her head, pausing for a moment before she continued and Trevor hated that she'd ever been in such a situation. He realized how lucky Joanna had been to be adopted so early. She could have ended up on the streets, too.

"I don't want to relive it all, but there were gangs of kids on the streets in those days. There probably still are. Some were into drugs and some were into petty thievery. Some were just lost souls. They lived under the expressways and there were enough predators that if you were alone, you really couldn't risk sleeping at night. In the daytime, though, people didn't want to see you around, sleeping or begging. I had a couple of bigger kids giving me trouble. I had no doubt what they wanted, so even though I wasn't sure what the old guy with the food wanted from me, I chose while I still could."

"But he didn't want sex from you?"

Chynna shook her head. "Nope. Not then. He was a protector, not a predator, although it took me a long time to believe it. I didn't know anything about tattoos then, but he gave me a place to sleep and a job. I became his assistant and he paid me as well as teaching me. It was his philosophy to pay it forward and help someone out—his younger partner at Mythos was another kid he'd found on the streets and helped five years before. The more I got to know Tristan, the more people I met who had been helped by him, usually when they'd pretty much given up hope."

"He had a reputation for compassion."

"Among other things," she said with an affectionate smile. "I'd never met anyone like him and I haven't since then either. He was physically big but also larger than life, with this booming laugh and an enthusiasm that had no bounds. He was fascinated by everything and everyone, yet he made every person who talked to him feel special. As if he was the sun, shining just for them."

Trevor nodded and smiled, knowing he didn't have that gift.

"He lived in the moment all the time. He was impulsive and passionate and wildly talented. Charming." She raised her brows. "Everyone loved him. He threw these incredible parties at the shop, because he owned the building and lived above it. I think he was familiar with every illicit substance known to mankind, as well as every kind of liquor and every kind of food, and he reveled in it all. He lived full out for every moment of every day, and I loved him so much for that. I wanted to be as engaged as he was, as much in love with life and sensation as he was."

"Of course you fell in love with him," Trevor said when she paused then made a joke. "I almost did when he was giving me this tattoo. He had a really magnetic personality."

She laughed and flicked a glance at Trevor. "Those were wild years, even though he wouldn't let me try a lot of things before I was eighteen. He was almost paternal, but I didn't want him to be a father to me. He thought I admired him, but I loved him, heart and soul."

Trevor wondered then whether there was any chance that Chynna would love again.

It might not have anything to do with him and his qualities: it might be the effect of Tristan's shadow.

She took a deep breath. "He taught me how to tattoo, but only after he saw that I could draw. He encouraged me to draw as much as possible and bought me supplies and I couldn't believe it when he wanted one of my drawings on his skin. It was a medusa, a beautiful woman who was also terrifying."

"I remember that," Trevor said. "It was on his left shoulder."

Chynna smiled, nodding. "It was. It was bigger than I'd intended to do it, but he insisted on everything being over the top. It took several sessions because I had things to learn, but he tutored me through it. Lots of people wanted one just because he had it, but I never did it the same way as his. He taught me that: to keep every work unique, to build a portfolio, to focus on one kind of image and explore variations. He launched me as an artist and I worked in his shop. It was only a matter of time before I seduced him, although I had to convince him that it wasn't just gratitude. The days and nights after I moved into his room were some of the happiest and most creative of my life. I thought my heart would burst when he asked me to marry him."

"I'm going to guess it wasn't a traditional ceremony."

"Not nearly. We went to city hall, then he hosted an enormous party, one that lasted three days and nights. That was when I first wondered if there would be a price to his lifestyle, but I was young and he was confident, and we carried on." She sighed. "They were gloriously happy times."

Trevor waited, sensing that there was another confession. When she didn't speak, he prompted her. "But?"

"But." Chynna smiled and shook her head. "Some people say that nothing lasts forever. I've always thought it could, but that didn't. Tristan designed a tattoo for me. It was a surprise and I knew he was really proud of it. It was big, a back piece, and he wanted to do it for me as an anniversary present." She turned to meet Tristan's gaze. "I didn't like the design. I thought it was more his style than mine, but he was insistent and we argued. He called me his muse. I felt..."

She tightened her lips and clenched the duvet. "I felt like he was trying to make me into something that suited him better than it suited me. I thought he was trying to define me, but I'd been there before and I'd survived that before, and it was the reason that I was on the street in the first place. I was never going to let another man tell me who and what I was, or what I should want to be because it suited him for me to play that role. We had an epic fight, our first and our last. When we'd finished yelling, I moved back into my old room and locked the door against him."

She shook her head. "He didn't come after me. He didn't force his way in—it was his house, after all—and he didn't beg for forgiveness. I cried myself to sleep and woke up to find that an envelope had been shoved beneath the door. It was late in the morning—we usually slept late—but the house was empty. Tristan had gone out, leaving me with that envelope."

Trevor was shocked. "He kicked you out?"

"Pretty much," Chynna said quietly and sighed. Her heartbreak was so obvious that Trevor didn't know what to say. He instinctively felt that Tristan had been unfair—they should have talked about it more—but doubted Chynna would see it that way.

Then he knew what to say. He'd just ask a practical question and hope it worked.

CHAPTER EIGHT

"What was in the envelope?"

"Money."

Trevor breathed a silent sigh of relief as Chynna began talking again.

She flicked a glance at him. "I mean thousands and thousands. Tristan did a lot of cash business and he kept it all at the house, although I was never sure where exactly. There wasn't a safe. I figured it was under floorboards or something. I wasn't sure I wanted to know, actually."

"Why would he do that?"

"He didn't trust banks. He called it institutionalized theft." She shrugged. "The note said that I should open my own shop, that it was time for me to take the next step. I didn't know whether that was an endorsement of my skills or a kick in the ass, but I was still so angry that I saw it as a rejection. If I couldn't have an opinion different from his, then I didn't want to stay. I took the money and my few things and I went down to Chinatown to rent a shop. I opened Imagination Ink, and eventually, I bought the building. I built a clientele and I found success, because of what Tristan had taught me. I brought in kids I found in the streets, because I knew I owed my life to Tristan's decision to do that. They didn't all stay, but some of them did, and some of them learned to be tattoo artists. I made two of them partners in Imagination Ink after Tristan died and ultimately sold it to one of them. Rox, who did my roses."

"Did Tristan know?"

"I never told him about it."

"Did he come there?"

"Not openly. He never crossed the threshold, as far as I knew. I used to think I saw him sometimes, late at night or early in the morning, standing across the street and looking, but I didn't speak to him until he was diagnosed."

"He called you then?"

She shook her head. "The kid he'd taken in called me. His name was Neo, or at least that's what he said it was. He'd heard about me: when Tristan got sick but wouldn't seek help, he called me, hoping I could change Tristan's mind."

"He disliked authority."

"He distrusted it. It was a learned response." Chynna stiffened. "So, I went up there, because I knew he wouldn't talk to me on the phone, and I could see right away how sick he was. He'd lost a lot of weight. He called me Persephone, the way he used to when he was talking about me being his muse. He tried to make a joke of the timeliness of my return and spit up blood when he tried to laugh. I didn't think it was funny."

"I don't get it."

"Persephone is a goddess, daughter of Demeter and the stolen bride of Hades. She governs true love, but she lives in the underworld with Hades so she facilitates communication with the dead. She can banish ghosts, I think by reasoning with them, and she's said to help with a painless death."

"Not funny," Trevor agreed.

Chynna shook her head. "I convinced him to go to a doctor, but the prognosis was as bad as we both expected. He had esophageal cancer and it was pretty advanced, probably because he'd been ignoring the signs." She looked down at her hands. "He declined treatment."

"Oh, Chynna."

She shook her head and her tears fell. "I took him back to his apartment over Mythos because it was what he wanted, and I took care of him because he'd taken care of me. We both knew it wouldn't be long. When he was asleep, I called his friends, asking them to come and see him one last time. He had a lot of company in those few weeks. The place could have had a revolving door. And we didn't talk much ourselves. There was always someone else to distract him from me." She sighed. "But he suffered so badly. It was terrible. He called it penance for his sins, but no one deserves what he endured. After one awful night, he asked me to come to bed with him. We spooned together the way we used to, but I was behind him, and I could feel that he was just bones. It made me cry. I held him and I knew I should apologize for that fight but before I could think of how to say it or how to begin, he slipped away. He kissed my hand and whispered 'thank you' and then he was gone. Just gone. I knew the instant that he died." Her tears fell then and Trevor held her close. "I never made it right," she confessed. "I had the chance and I didn't take it and I'll regret that for the rest of my life."

She cried a bit then but less than Trevor expected. He didn't know what to say. He knew plenty about having regrets but not about making them go away.

She straightened eventually and wiped away her tears, forcing a smile for him. "Sorry."

"Don't apologize."

"He's been gone ten years," she whispered. "Sometimes it seems like a lifetime ago and sometimes it seems like yesterday."

Trevor just nodded.

Chynna took a deep breath. "I ended up with the job of cleaning out his things. He'd told me where there was an envelope but I hadn't opened it when he was alive. It had his will in it, and it had been done by a lawyer, all the t's crossed and the i's dotted. He'd left everything to his daughter, who lived in California near his ex-wife. She came and she was about my age, but so angry and disdainful of her father and his abilities. I suggested an auction of Tristan's things to raise money for cancer research or a resource for homeless kids, but she refused. She said she was going to chuck everything and sell the shop. Some developer wanted to buy it and tear it down, as part of a plan to fill the block with condominiums. Neo knew where the cash was hidden, although we'd spent a lot of it on living expenses and there'd been no revenue while Tristan was sick. I gave him some of it before surrendering the rest to her and I don't regret that. I gave away his drawings and few possessions to his friends, who I knew would cherish any keepsake."

"And you?"

"I took only the envelope with my name on it which had been in the bigger envelope along with the will." She shook her head. "My name isn't Chynna. Not really. That's the name I took when I ran away. The name I was given when I was born was Elizabeth. Tristan was the last person who knew that, and he addressed the envelope to Elizabeth, not Chynna."

"What was in it?"

"The drawing for that back piece." She smiled. "And a note from him about what it meant. I'd totally misunderstood him. He wasn't defining me. He understood me. It was about where I'd been and where he thought I was going, a kind of a talisman for a safe journey. I realized that he'd known he would die before me and had always intended for me to move on, that he didn't believe he was my future. He just thought he was someone to help me on my way. I was angry with him for not seeing more potential in us, but also I was angry with myself for not asking what the drawing meant when he'd first given it to me."

"What happened to it?"

"I have the sketch and the letter. I've thought about getting it done, but he should have been the one to give it to me. It would have had his *chi* in it then." She sighed and forced a smile. "But it's too late now. There. Now you know my story." She would have risen from the bed, but Trevor caught her hand in his.

"Why don't you want your grief to heal?"

"Because I don't deserve it. I didn't listen to him. I didn't trust him."

"He trusted you. You took care of him and he let you. You were there for him at the end."

She lifted her gaze to Trevor's. "Was it me or was it his muse?"

"Weren't you one and the same to him?"

"I guess." She shrugged. "Taking care of him seemed like the least I could do. We were married, after all."

"Maybe it was just the first thing you could do."

"What do you mean?"

"Is it time for a memorial tattoo?"

She considered the idea, her lips pursed. "It just might be. I have to think about it a little more."

"Where does the bird come in?"

Chynna laughed and he was relieved by the sight. "I have a friend who works at an animal rescue. They get a lot of exotic pets. People change their minds once the novelty wears off. There was this raven, who'd been raised from a chick and hand-fed. He didn't know how to hunt or interact with other birds, let alone survive in the wild, even though he was an adult. He became too big and too mischievous for the person who had raised him, so he was surrendered. My friend thinks everyone needs a pet and she thought I needed an unusual one. Tristan had died and I'd sold the shop to Rox and I was at loose ends a bit. I went to see the raven, although I was very skeptical, and I just lost my heart. He has this gleam in his eyes and you just know he's going to make trouble. He wanted Tristan's ring from my hand, which is how he got that name."

"Did you give it to him?"

"It's in his hoard. He has a little collection of shiny things and likes to rearrange them, or maybe show them off. He asks me questions and loves watching old movies."

"Questions?"

"We've gotten to understand each other. Either he speaks English or I speak raven." She smiled. "He chooses tarot cards and he's pretty good at it. I feel like he's in touch with the hidden side of the world, just like Tristan was." She looked up. "Plus he reminds me how wonderful the world is, each and every day."

"It sounds like Tristan is a good name for him."

She wrinkled her nose. "I kind of miss him, actually. Crazy bird."

"How long do ravens live?"

"My friend said ten or fifteen years in the wild, but they can live up to forty years in captivity." Chynna smiled. "I'm probably stuck with him for the duration, but that's fine by me. He's good company."

Trevor nodded and leaned back in the bed. Chynna stretched out beside him in her fluffy robe and they held hands.

"Thank you," he said. "That's a heck of a story."

"Thank you," she replied and squeezed his hand. "I actually feel better for sharing it."

Trevor was exhausted but there was one more thing he needed to ask her. He rolled to his side and looked down at her. Her gaze fell, predictably, to his tattoo. "So, what's the difference?" he asked quietly and her gaze flew to his. "What's the difference between me being rootless and you being rooted? We've both let the past shape our present. We both want a different future, but we haven't done anything to change that."

Her smile was slow and lit her entire face. "There is no difference. It's something else we have in common. But we're both making changes now." She rolled him to his back and laid on top of him. She framed his face in her hands and looked down at him. "Here's to the transformative road trip," she whispered, then kissed him before he could reply.

And that was just fine by Trevor.

It was amazing how just sharing a story could make Chynna feel so much better. She felt lighter on her feet and her heart seemed to be filled with promise. Trevor was gone and there was a note beside the alarm clock.

POOL'S OPEN

Below that, he'd noted the time of his departure. He'd been gone an hour so Chynna suspected he was finished with his swim. She wasn't in a hurry to swim naked and alone, since there were more guests in the hotel, plus she was hungry. Chynna washed and left her room, not really surprised to find him in a suit at the front desk.

He definitely cleaned up well.

He winked at her before helping some departing guests to carry their luggage out to their car, which was idling right outside the door. There was Christmas music playing and for the first time in a long time, Chynna listened to it. She was tempted to sing along. Trevor strode back inside, gave an elaborate shiver and then came straight to her.

"Okay?" he asked and she smiled.

"Better than okay. I'm ready to take on the world."

"Excellent. Merry Christmas, by the way." He stole a kiss that became long and leisurely. His hand was on the back of her waist, lifting her toward him, and he kissed her as if they had all the time in the world.

Chynna stepped back reluctantly, then ran a hand down his chest. "Merry Christmas to you, too," she said and his smile flashed.

"It's definitely one to remember."

"Why did you talk to me when I first arrived?" she asked on impulse.

"Is that one of your questions?"

"It could be."

"That's easy. Because you look like you have it all together. Like you know what you want. I find that very very sexy."

His answer surprised Chynna but she liked it. "I thought you were going to say that you noticed me because you'd decided it was time to find someone."

"Maybe that was part of it. Either way, I have no complaints." He smiled down at her. "You?"

"Not one."

A frown touched Trevor's brow and Chynna sensed there was something he hadn't told her.

"What's wrong?"

"Nothing." He smiled again. "I want to talk to you about something but we'll do it when there's more time." He nodded toward another couple who were headed for the front desk with their luggage.

Chynna tried to ignore her sense of foreboding. "When you're unemployed?" she asked lightly instead.

"Good plan." He grinned. "Spencer's cooking this morning, so you don't have to work for your breakfast."

Chynna laughed. "I didn't mind." She indicated that he should go and watched him greet the guests. He asked after their stay as he checked them out and she admired his easy charm again. Then she went in for breakfast, making a plan for her contribution to the wedding feast.

Maybe roasted vegetables. They'd need side vegetables for the turkey and someone was probably already doing potatoes. Reyna would make something wonderful for dessert. She resolved to check with Spencer and followed the smell of coffee to the kitchen, humming along to *Hark the Herald Angels Sing*.

Gabe thought the feast at Jane's was the perfect culmination of their Christmas wedding. He was glad that Spencer and Liv were together, and was certain of the future of the lodge. The simple reality was that with both partners married, there was less possibility of radical change in their situations. He felt badly about Trevor, but his old friend and former partner was easygoing about it. He knew Trevor would land on his feet.

To Gabe's pleasure, Daphne and Ned had decided to stay on. He and Lexi had planned to spend a few days in New York with them before they headed home. Ned's kids had never seen snow and earlier in the morning, Kade had introduced them to snowball fights. They'd started to build snow forts while everyone else was cooking and it had been hard to drag them inside to change in time to get to Jane's.

Gabe drove his SUV with Lexi, Daphne, Ned and the kids, along with a supply of wine in the back. He'd brought wines for every course from the wine cellar at the lodge, knowing that it couldn't be any other way at Spencer's wedding celebration. Spencer had gone with Liv to pick up his mom and Katerina, who had retreated to the family home once the power had come back on there. Reyna and Kade had driven into town to collect Clem, the bookseller and Penny, who owned the thrift store, at Chynna's suggestion. They both tended to spend the holiday alone and Gabe was glad that Chynna had thought about including them. Trevor had offered to pick up Liv's mom in town and Chynna was with him.

Eighteen people meant a serious feast.

The smell of roast turkey had greeted them on arrival at the oldest house in town, and Jane had clearly been excited to have so many guests. She'd also been a bit flustered, and Spencer had taken charge of the kitchen with her permission.

"It'll be a bit crowded at the table," Jane said, but Gabe and Trevor exchanged a glance. "That's why I didn't set it yet."

"We'll take care of it," Trevor said with authority. "Your dishes are all in the sideboard."

"And some in the pantry." She showed him around and Trevor took charge. "I want to use all the good china, silver and crystal," she said firmly. "It's Christmas. I don't care if I'm washing up into the new year."

"You won't have to," Chynna said. "We'll help."

Gabe poured Jane a glass of sherry and invited her to sit and enjoy her guests. Her relief was evident. Daphne asked Jane about the age of the house while Reyna took people's coats into the parlor and encouraged them to leave their boots in the hall. There was holiday music playing somewhere but the sound of happy conversation quickly overwhelmed it. The house was decked with greenery and plaid bows, and looked wonderful. Fires crackled on the hearths in both living room and parlor.

Everyone was taking a jar of honey home from Honey Hill. There was a line of jars on the table in the foyer of the house, each dressed with a Christmas bow.

The kitchen was filled with helping hands and Jane's golden retriever happily wove her way through the crowd, tail wagging like a banner. The bride didn't wear white, but she had on a pretty peasant dress with embroidered bees down the bodice. Gabe had never seen Liv in a dress and guessed that Lexi had loaned it to her.

Gabe made sure everyone had a drink, then went to check on the preparations. He found Trevor and Chynna in the large dining room, arranging chairs around. It was a massive carved table which looked to be cherry and also antique. Maybe the room had been built around it. There was already a beautiful white damask tablecloth on it.

"It's a huge table," Trevor said as Gabe came into the dining room.

"Thank goodness," Chynna said. "We can all eat together."

"Nicer than a buffet," Trevor agreed.

The room had striped wallpaper and large windows on two walls. There was a silver tea service on the sideboard, wound with Christmas greens, a chandelier hanging over the table and sconces on the walls. There were a number of candlesticks on the sideboard too, all filled with beeswax candles.

Trevor eased a kitchen chair in at the side, between the chairs that matched the table. It was slightly narrower. "Two at each end, seven down each side? It should be five down each side and one at each end, but we can squeeze a little."

"It'll be worth it," Chynna said. "How about Spencer and Liv at the head of the table," she suggested and Gabe nodded.

"The moms at the foot of the table," he said. "Katerina beside Spencer's mom."

Trevor nodded. "We can't do bride's side and groom's side, really, but we can alternate men and women. Almost."

Jane had set out little silver holders to designate places on the sideboard, along with some blank tags. Chynna had already written the name of each guest on one of the cards in a beautiful script and was fitting the cards into the holders.

"That looks like old advertisements," Gabe said, noting her skill.

"Or tattoos," she said with a smile.

Trevor began to place them as they'd discussed. Lexi was beside Spencer, then Gabe, then Daphne, the two kids and Ned. That filled one side with Katerina. Kade was seated beside Liv, then Reyna, Clem the bookseller, Chynna, Trevor, Penny and Jane.

"Close," Chynna said when he was done. "Just one woman too many."

"Don't say that," Trevor teased. "I thought she and Liv's mom might know each other."

Gabe nodded. "Of course. And it'll be easier for the kids to be with Ned and Daphne."

Once they agreed on the seating, Trevor opened the sideboard. The array of china was impressive. It was all bone china with a gold border. They decided upon chargers, with dinner plates and soup bowls, bread and butter plates to one side and plates for dessert on the sideboard. Gabe found red and white wine glasses, water glasses, and put the liqueur glasses and brandy snifters on the sideboard. Chynna opened the silver drawers and caught her breath.

"It's all polished," she said with awe.

"Jane said she wants to use it."

"We have to help her with the washing up," Chynna said then chose salad forks and soup spoons, knives and forks for the main course, dessert forks and spoons and coffee spoons. Meanwhile, Gabe checked with Spencer about serving plates and silver, and they got all that sorted out. Things were getting busy in the kitchen and the volume of noise was rising along with the delicious smells.

Chynna was putting the candles on the table when Gabe checked on the dining room, along with a centerpiece of greenery. "It looks like a magazine shoot," Reyna said with approval from the doorway and took a picture of it. Daphne peeked around her shoulder and did the same, then Spencer called that it was time to eat.

They sat down almost at the stroke of noon, winter sunlight streaming through the windows and the table almost groaning at the weight of their glorious meal. Jane said Grace and Gabe took Lexi's hand, knowing he would never forget.

Then he lifted his glass and toasted the happy couple.

Honey Hill.

Reyna smiled as Kade drove into town after their Christmas celebration at Jane's. The town really was picture-perfect, and even more perfect since she'd met Kade there. She felt full and warm and happy, and was barely listening to Penny's excited summary of events from the back seat. Clem grunted at intervals from beside her, and that seemed to be enough to keep her talking.

The snow had stopped and even though it was only four, it was getting dark already. They'd stayed at Chynna's insistence to wash up all of the dishes, and had left Jane with the clean ones on the dining room table, ready to be put away. The kitchen had been sparkling when they left, and Jane had packed leftovers for some of the guests. Everyone had taken home Reyna's Christmas cupcakes.

They drove past the church on the corner with the nativity scene set up in front, one light burning above the manger like that long-ago beckoning star. The figures, Reyna knew, had been carved by the owner of the general store decades before and were lovingly set up each year. She waved to Mary and Joseph as she always did and saw Kade smile.

She saw as they turned onto the main street that the fairy lights in the holiday decorations were already lit. Each shop had cedar roping draped over the front window, many with fairy lights wound into the branches, and big plaid bows blowing in the wind. With the freshly-fallen snow, the town looked like it should star in a holiday movie.

Honey Hill for the Holidays.
Coming Home for Christmas.
I Found my Heart in Honey Hill.

Reyna slanted a glance at Kade, who was concentrating on his driving. The roads had to be slippery and she didn't want to distract him. She studied his profile, liking how intent he was on doing his best all the time. No wonder he'd stolen her heart away. He was all the good stuff and being with him made her happier than she'd ever believed she had the right to be.

He stopped in front of the shop she'd sold to Lexi and Gabe, the tires crunching in the snow.

Cupcake Heaven had had an extreme make-over, from cute pink pastry shop to slick art gallery. One of Lexi's paintings was displayed in the front window, a winter scene that conveyed an awe of nature's majesty in a very few brush strokes. The architectural details of the original Victorian house that Reyna had restored were still maintained, but the palette was more subdued. She knew the house was in good hands. Its holiday decorations were in shades of silver and white, and even the cedar roping looked elegant and urban.

On the right side was the thrift store that Penny had taken over from her mom. It was one of Reyna's favorite places to shop since Penny had brought in a large inventory of vintage clothing. Penny had a gift for finding unique pieces and also for repairing those garments in need of a touch or two. She was teaching sewing classes in the workroom of the shop and her business was thriving.

"Thanks for the ride!" she said when she stepped out into the snow. "It was a fabulous meal. That might have been the biggest roast turkey I've ever seen."

"I'm glad you could come," Reyna said, getting out to embrace her former neighbor.

"Of course. It was the best. And I have leftovers!" Penny laughed. "My favorite part of Christmas dinners is the leftover turkey sandwich the next day. Thank you!" She blew Kade a kiss and headed toward her shop, keys jingling.

Reyna could smell woodfires burning and heard a dog barking across the street. It was Doc Maitland's lab and Reyna could see the dog's face in the window.

"Nice of you to think of us," Clem said gruffly, offering his hand. "Merry Christmas, Reyna." The older man owned the bookstore to the left of the former Cupcake Heaven and lived there alone.

Reyna hugged him, knowing he'd never initiate an embrace but would tolerate one. "Merry Christmas, Clem. I suppose you're going to spend the evening with a good book."

"You'd better believe it," he said with a grin.

"Which will be?"

"Gibbon's *History of the Decline and Fall of the Roman Empire*," he said with satisfaction. He looked like he was itching to get back to it.

"Doesn't sound very festive."

"To each his or her own, Reyna. I like an opinionated historian, so Gibbon is a favorite." He cleared his throat. *"The various modes of worship which prevailed in the Roman world were all considered by the people as equally true; by the philosophers as equally false; and by the magistrate as equally useful."* Clem winked at Reyna then waved to Kade. "Good night to both of you, and thank you for the invitation." He held up the box he carried. Reyna knew there were three cupcakes inside, because she'd packed it for him. "There's nothing like a sweet with a sip of brandy on a winter night like this. Thank you again, Reyna, and thank you, Kade for the ride." Kade waved.

"Merry Christmas to both of you."

"Merry Christmas, Clem." Reyna kissed his cheek, then got back into the van. Kade drove around the corner and parked in the driveway of the house his aunt and uncle had bought and restored for their retirement. The lights were on in the house and Reyna could hear the Christmas music playing.

Kade turned off the engine but didn't get out of the van. "That was nice today."

"It was. I liked seeing everyone together." She noticed that he didn't seem to be in a hurry to go into the house. Reyna didn't mind. It had been a hectic few days and she liked having Kade to herself, if only for a moment. His aunt and uncle were kind and hospitable, but she'd be glad to get back to their own place in Portland. She reached out and touched his hand, thinking of how they might celebrate that.

Kade took off his glove and claimed her hand. "It's been a busy holiday this year."

"It has." She waited, guessing he had something to say.

He gave her an intent look. "Everyone married but you."

"Yes. All the heart tattoos have delivered. Even Chynna looks like she's found a partner."

"Does it bother you that Lexi and Liv are married but you're not?"

Reyna shook her head. "I've never been one to follow the crowd."

"Does that mean you don't want to get

married?"

She smiled, hoping this was leading where she wanted it to go. "It means that there's a right time for everyone. I'll be glad to get married at the right time to the right man."

"How will you know?"

"I'll know." She spoke with confidence but noticed his quick frown. "Don't you think you'll know?"

"Absolutely. I already do." He turned his hand over and held on to hers, his gaze fixed upon her. "I just never know what you're thinking."

"Don't actions speak louder than words?"

"Usually. Sometimes, though, it's good to hear the words." He was watching her, his eyes dark.

Reyna leaned closer. "Any particular words?"

"Just three. And then four."

Reyna smiled. "I love you."

"That's three," he murmured, leaning forward to touch his lips to hers. Reyna's heart leapt right on cue. "I love you," he whispered against her mouth then kissed her.

"What four?" she asked when he finally lifted his head. The windows were steamed up but she didn't care. Her heart was skipping and she felt just as flustered as she had the very first time he'd ever kissed her. This man. Oh, he was the one for her.

"Will you marry me?" he asked, his gaze locked with hers. "Or is it too soon?"

"That's four and five," she whispered. "I like four better."

Kade smiled.

Reyna reached up to touch his cheek. "But I only need one. Or maybe two."

He looked slightly alarmed, which made her smile.

"Yes, please," she whispered and he grinned before he caught her close and kissed her again.

When they parted, they were both breathless and the windows were completely fogged. "I thought we could choose rings together," he said.

"I know just the ones," Reyna said, savoring his surprise. She laughed. "I was going to propose to you at New Year's."

Kade chuckled and kissed her again. "Why do I have the feeling that you'll always be keeping me on my toes?"

"Why do I get the feeling that you don't mind?"

"Because I don't," he said with satisfaction. "I wouldn't have it any other way."

Who could have guessed when she'd gone to New York with Liv and Lexi that things would work out so well and so quickly for all of them? Chynna really had summoned some magic for all of them. Reyna was glad there had been a bit of it left for Chynna, too. Seeing her and Trevor together made it easy to guess the resolution of that story, and it pleased Reyna enormously. She smiled at Kade and squeezed his hand and he muttered something about a lack of privacy that made her laugh.

Kade gave her a hot look, then got out of the

van, coming around to open her door for her. She stepped out into his arms and a very satisfying kiss, then they looked up at the darkening sky together. The stars were coming out, twinkling far overhead, and she sighed with contentment. She was exactly where she needed to be.

"The winter solstice is the darkest day of the year," Reyna said, holding tightly to Kade. "From here, every day gets a little bit brighter. I feel like I met you when I was coming out of my own darkness, and the future has just gotten brighter and brighter." She smiled at him. "There was a time when I would have been afraid to tie my life to anyone else's, but you helped me move beyond that. I think it's only fair that we end up together as a result."

"I like the sound of that," Kade said and kissed her one last time before they went in to share the news with his aunt and uncle.

It was the best Christmas Chynna had enjoyed in a very long time. In fact, it was the only Christmas she'd enjoyed in years. Since Tristan's death, she'd been surviving the day—this year, she savored every moment. It was wonderful to be with old friends and new ones, celebrating marriages, enjoying each other's company and good food, too.

They got back to the lodge and she knew she couldn't eat one more bite. She went back to her room to change into something more comfortable and considered her roses in her reflection.

Under the Mistletoe

It was time for a fresh start, and as always, Chynna wanted to celebrate that in ink.

She got out her tattoo gun and chose red ink. She studied the roses on her left arm, then touched some color into the middle of one petal on her forearm. She put down the gun and rubbed the tattoo, knowing the look she wanted. She'd shade the petal, making it darkest at the center of the flower, plus make the flowers darker as they rose to her shoulders. It was a bit arduous since she could only work with one hand, but she was making progress on that petal when there was a tap at her door.

It was Trevor, but this time, he was dressed in jeans.

He looked just as good dressed down as dressed up. Maybe better, since his T-shirt let her see that fantastic tattoo.

"Unemployed?" she asked with a smile.

"I'm a free man." His gaze dropped to her left arm. "Are you hurt?"

She glanced down and realized the red might look like blood. "No, it's ink. I have an idea, but I could use some help."

"I'm yours to command."

"Can you wipe when I ask you to?"

"Sure."

"I just want to do the one flower, to see how I like it."

"Won't it look odd to have only one with color?"

"Once I get it right, I'll let Rox do the rest to match."

He sat and did as she instructed, watching her work for a while. It was nice to be together, a hum of awareness coupled with an ease with each other's company. "Is this your memorial tattoo?" he finally asked.

"No," Chynna said. "That's next." She took a deep breath. "I'm going to get Rox to do the back piece that Tristan designed for me. It'll be a big project. I want it to look like the color is emanating from it and dripping into my roses."

"So, they'll be darker at the shoulder and paler at the wrist."

She nodded, liking that he understood. "And the back piece will be in full color."

"It'll be spectacular."

"I know."

"And the color gradation is because..." he invited, although she guessed he knew.

"Because Tristan was the sun, the center of my world and the reason I found my way. He lit my path in more ways than one and that influence is a big part of commemorating our partnership."

Trevor nodded and frowned a little, his gaze dropping to her tattoo. He watched her work for a while, wiping the ink at her gesture, and she had the sense that he was choosing his words.

"You said earlier that you were going to tell me something," she invited finally.

"It's not that I want to keep secrets. I just don't

know whether it's better to tell you or not. I don't want you to feel pressured or that I'm hiding things."

Chynna smiled. "Sounds like the best option is to tell me. I'll try not to feel either."

He nodded once. "I have a job offer."

"Wow, that was fast." She noticed that he didn't look very excited about it. "Isn't it a good one?"

"It's a great one. It's exactly what I said I wanted."

Chynna noticed the qualification but didn't comment on it yet. "Kind of like Wolfe Lodge."

"A lot like Wolfe Lodge. It's a hotel with restaurants, a new project with a great location. I can buy in at the ground, be a partner, probably be settled for the duration there. Lots of challenge and opportunity. Good people who I already know and trust."

"But," Chynna said, hearing his lack of enthusiasm.

"But." Trevor took a breath and met her gaze steadily, watching her reaction. "It's in Hawaii."

Chynna's heart stopped. She knew she didn't hide her surprise but tried to smile. All along she'd been insisting to Trevor that this was just a fling, but now that there was a prospect of him vanishing from her life, and soon, she didn't want him to go. She felt shaken, but wanted to think about her reaction before she talked about it. "How could Hawaii be a negative?" she asked lightly.

"Well, it's a long way from New York." As usual,

Trevor wasn't shy or coy. He put his question right on the table and Chynna liked knowing exactly where she stood. He shook his head. "I know it's way too early to ask questions about any future we might have so I'm not going to. I also know that just a week ago, I would have been changing my flight reservation right this minute as I drove to the airport."

"Your flight reservation?"

"Mike asked me to come out and have a look in January, once I was done here," Trevor explained. "He sent me a ticket for the 10th."

That seemed so soon. Chynna frowned as she added more color to the petal.

"The thing is I always go," Trevor said, his voice low. "I'm always footloose and ready to relocate. I just don't feel in such a hurry this time. I want to know more about you. I mean, we haven't come close to finishing our agreed twenty questions." He smiled and so did Chynna. "But at the same time, I don't want you to feel cornered or on the spot. I just want to keep flowing along, seeing where this leads."

"Maybe it doesn't lead anywhere," Chynna felt compelled to say. "Maybe the magic was just about these past few days, time out of time." She had a hard time believing that even as she said the words.

"Maybe. A free pass is a powerful thing."

"Even transformative."

He nodded. "But don't you want to know for sure instead of guessing?"

She couldn't say it out loud, but she did. "People have long distance relationships." She was surprised in one way that she even suggested the possibility, yet in another way, she wasn't. It felt right to be with Trevor.

He scoffed. "That's a compromise and I don't think it's a good one."

"How so?"

"People have long distance relationships because they don't want to commit to what's going on. Ultimately, I have to think it dooms everything. At some point, it becomes clear that the two parties are choosing work or family or something over the relationship. And that becomes an issue when one of the two parties wants more." Chynna put down the tattoo gun and he wiped her skin, the weight of his hand lingering on her arm as he studied her tattoo. "I like to be in or out."

"Black or white."

"Committed or leaving all parties free to carry on."

"No compromises."

He smiled and shrugged. "I think relationships need more to survive, let alone thrive."

Chynna had to admit that she agreed with him. She still kept silent.

"And I already want more. For me, going to Hawaii means we're stepping away from each other for good."

"All or nothing makes it high stakes."

"Exactly. Which is why I didn't mention it right

away. I had to think about what was the best plan, but the truth is I don't know. I just wanted to be honest with you."

"Thank you." Chynna kissed him. "I appreciate that."

"So, lady's choice. Option one is that we still do the road trip to New York."

"And make the most of this interval," Chynna said.

"While option two is that I take you to the train station in Portland, wave goodbye and head to the airport to change my booking to Honolulu."

He waited, giving her the choice. Since he'd explained what he wanted and she felt as if his departure would mean losing the best opportunity to come her way in a long time, that meant there wasn't one.

"I think you just became a limited time offer," Chynna said. "And I think we should make the most of every moment."

"I knew I liked the way you thought."

"We're not nearly done with diminishing the power of shit anniversaries," Chynna said with resolve as she put down the tattoo gun. "Not only do I want to take that road trip with you, but I think we should spend New Year's Eve together in New York. Come stay with me and meet my pet raven. I'll get you through your anniversary, just like you got me through mine."

She wouldn't have guessed that she'd make the invitation but it felt right.

She took a breath. "And then we'll see where we are."

Trevor laughed and put down the cloth. "You are amazing," he said with such obvious admiration that Chynna found herself smiling, too. He spared a glance upward. "But you need some mistletoe in this room."

"You don't need an excuse to kiss me," she replied.

"You're exactly right," he purred, then kissed her so deeply that she forgot about her tattoo for a long while.

She was too busy savoring the moment.

CHAPTER NINE

They left the lodge together the next morning, everything loaded in Trevor's Jeep. He and Chynna had gone for an early morning swim, naked in the lodge pool, and no one knew the difference. He was so relieved that his confession hadn't caused a crisis between them. In fact, it seemed to have made her more inquisitively passionate, as if she really did intend to make every minute count. Trevor was falling hard and he didn't care. He'd meet her challenges and answer her questions and hope for the best.

Chynna looked fabulous and urban, and now he knew that she didn't just look like the kind of woman he wanted to be with—she was the one.

It was December 26. He had one week in her company. He didn't like having a romance with a deadline, but he also didn't like waffling over decisions.

He shook hands with Gabe and they all wished each other well, then headed out. The roads were clear and it was a cold sunny day. On either side of the road, the snow sparkled like crystals. They drove in companionable silence for a while, then Chynna spoke. "Best job ever?" she asked and Trevor smiled.

"Easy. Bill's diner. The first one was the best. You?"

"When Tristan hired me as a tattoo artist at Mythos."

"Why?"

"Because I realized I was an artist and that I could create something that would endure. Maybe something that would make a change in the world. That was pretty empowering."

"Life goal?" he asked.

She answered without hesitation. "To leave the world a better place than it would be without me."

"Nice. I like that."

"Come on. Your turn."

"To see everyone who crosses my threshold better fed than they were the day before."

Chynna laughed at that and the sound made him smile.

"Favorite dinner?"

"Steak frites." Again, she didn't hesitate.

"I like that you're decisive."

"You were right. I know what I like." She shook a finger at him. "Bonus if there's fresh aioli."

"I know just the place."

"What about you?"

"Fish tacos with fresh guacamole." He nodded. "And I know just the place. Tomorrow for lunch."

Trevor had booked a room in a boutique hotel in the Old Port area of Portland and Chynna loved it. The streets were cobbled and the buildings were restored. It was decorated for the holidays and they went shopping after they checked in. She bought gifts for everyone in New York and a few things for herself, glad she didn't have to figure out how to carry it all home on the train. They stopped in a church when they heard carols being sung and joined in. They walked to look at the ocean and ducked into coffee shops and restaurants when they needed to get out of the wind.

Trevor knew the city well and was an excellent tour guide. He also knew someone at every restaurant, apparently, and it seemed that everyone liked and respected him. Chynna listened to some reminiscing and some shop talk and didn't mind at all. She heard him ask about business and about popular choices, and knew he was gathering information. She also saw how glad people were to have him stop by and knew her impression of his character was right. It was good to see Trevor in his element.

They had steak frites in a cozy bistro, then made love, falling asleep spooned together under a duvet.

He turned the tables on her the second day and

asked about tattoo artists she knew in town. She knew a few and found some more, hunting down shops and talking to other artists, pointing out their work. Some knew her by reputation or association, and it was nice to make new connections. They had fish tacos and there was a piece on the television about F5. She told him about the club and the partners, then they watched the pop-ups that had aired so far on her phone.

The day was over too quickly.

They decided to stay another day and skip Boston, spending Friday driving to New York. They reached New York in the afternoon and Trevor arranged for a parking spot at a local garage. They carried everything up to Chynna's studio apartment, then went to F5 to pick up Tristan, the raven. Chynna hunted down Theo in the office. She left Trevor in the tattoo shop, then went up to Theo's apartment with him to get Tristan. The raven was so delighted to see her that he turned away from the movie—*Swing Time*, his very favorite—to fly across the space to greet her. She laughed as he rubbed his beak on her hand and made so many sounds that Theo laughed.

"It's like he's trying to update you on everything that's happened while you were gone."

"He probably is." Chynna considered Theo and noticed a new vitality about him. Tristan, apparently disliking that he wasn't the focus of her attention, picked something out of his trinket box and presented it to Chynna. It was a silver cufflink.

"How did you get that again?" Theo demanded and the bird cackled with glee. "He's unbelievable."

"He is." Chynna laughed and gave the cufflink back to Theo.

"And I've seen enough Ginger Rogers and Fred Astaire movies to last me a while."

"I'm sure."

"Good trip?"

"Great trip. The wedding was lovely, and it was probably good that the weather kept me away for a few extra days."

"And you have company."

"I do." Chynna blushed as Theo smiled. She gave him the thank-you gift she'd brought for him. It was a gift package from Wolfe Lodge with local honey from Jane, some chevre from a local producer and a conserve from Spencer's kitchen. "All you need is a baguette."

"Thank you, but you didn't have to bring me anything."

"I did." She didn't want to ask about the tattoo, but she had a feeling it was making a difference. "How are you?"

"Good. Tired. These pop-ups are fun but a bit brutal."

"Is that all?"

"What do you mean?" Theo was a private person and Chynna knew it.

She shrugged. "Isn't this the first Christmas you didn't go home to England?"

"It is and it's been too busy for me to get

sentimental," he said with a shake of his head. "Everyone else knows so you're bound to hear about it. I'll tell you my big news on the way back downstairs."

They packed up Tristan's few things—his trinket box, his food and his perch—and the bird flew to the elevator doors and back to Chynna's shoulder when they opened the apartment door, clearly understanding what was going on. Theo told her about his college girlfriend reappearing in his life and that they had a son he hadn't known about until this week, and Chynna just listened.

"I'm sure it will work out well," she said, hoping it would.

Theo nodded. "Me, too." He shook hands with Trevor when she introduced them and Trevor asked a few questions about the club. When Theo left, Tristan whistled after Theo.

"He says thanks," Chynna called. "And so do I."

Tristan made his quorling sound and nodded with enthusiasm, then went to his trinket box to rummage. Chynna laughed when she saw that he had the second silver cufflink in there. "You are a troublemaker," she informed him. He had a way of looking at her as if he was raising one brow in surprise and he did that now. Chynna laughed then rubbed his beak. He closed his eyes. "And yes, I missed you, too." She kissed the top of his head, then took the cufflink to Theo.

She returned to find Trevor watching Tristan with his tarot cards. The bird had obviously communicated that he wanted the deck on the counter and Trevor had moved it for him. The raven walked across the cards and the counter, croaking to himself as he spread them out with his feet. Maybe he was arranging them. They were all face down, so maybe he was feeling for the energy of the right card. There was no telling how he chose. Chynna crossed the floor, intrigued.

"Does he do this often?" Trevor asked.

"All the time. The tarot cards are his thing."

"Wait. He *reads* tarot cards?"

"He chooses them and I read them. He's pretty good at it, actually." She waited as he arranged the cards to his satisfaction, then pulled one loose with his beak. He shoved it aside and took the one that had been beneath it, then offered it to Chynna, his eyes bright. "This one's for me?" she asked and he bobbed his head once she accepted it.

It was The Magician, the first card of the higher arcana, a card that Tristan often pulled for creators and artists, and it was right side up. Tristan chattered away after that, quorling and croaking, as fulsome as she'd ever heard him, then pecked at the card and watched her. He seemed to be explaining it, or admonishing her.

The Magician was about accomplishing something, applying and asserting oneself, achieving goals and ambitions. It was a card about taking the initiative and creating change.

Chynna couldn't help thinking that it was about her and Trevor, and how the choice was hers.

Interesting.

"Sounds important," Trevor said. He couldn't see which card she held from where he stood and Chynna was aware that he was watching her.

Tristan made his rolling sound and returned to his cards, kicking them around until he chose another one. This time, he presented it to Trevor, who took it and turned it over. "The Fool," he said, reading the card, then smiled. "That doesn't seem like a vote of confidence."

"It's a great card, actually," Chynna said. "I often think it's the most powerful one in the deck."

"Really?"

"It's the null card and when you add a zero to anything..."

"It becomes ten times more." Trevor nodded.

"The Fool means fresh starts." Chynna went to stand beside him. "See? He's setting out to find his fortune and is ready for an adventure. This card often indicates a new job or a new investment."

"Or a new relationship?" Trevor asked.

"Absolutely. A change."

"And yours?"

"The Magician. It's about energy and achievement, about attaining goals or making the first move. It's about being the prime mover and making things happen."

"Making magic, maybe?"

Chynna laughed. "It can feel like that." She glanced up and found him watching her, his gaze warm. He might have said something but he didn't.

Instead, he bent and kissed her, sweet and hot and demanding, until his phone rang and they reluctantly drew apart. Tristan had started to rummage in his hoard, his cards forgotten.

"Trevor Graham," he said, keeping his hand on Chynna's waist. She put Tristan's cards into a stacked deck again, not wanting to eavesdrop on the conversation. Then Trevor straightened. "Joanna?" he whispered as if he couldn't believe it. When Chynna looked up, he grinned. *"Joanna!"* he mouthed to her, his eyes alight, and she was so glad.

When she turned, Tristan landed on her shoulder again. His claws dug in a little bit, but she was used to that. She assumed he wanted a bit of affection and raised her hand to stroke his feathers, but he bent down and tugged at the chain around her neck. He made a sound like a question and she lifted the ring on the chain, holding it in her palm. He tried to claim it, as he had many times before, but this time, Chynna knew the raven was right.

It was time for her to make a move and shape her future.

She took the ring off the chain, aware that Trevor was watching her, and gave it to the bird. Tristan made a croak of triumph and flew across the shop, tucking it securely into the trinket box of his hoard as he chirped quietly to himself.

When Chynna looked back at Trevor, he'd averted his gaze, obviously concentrating on Joanna's words. How could she ask him to turn down the opportunity he'd wanted?

It was a short but wonderful phone call. Trevor quickly learned that his sister had a habit of interrupting people in her excitement. He didn't feel like he had a chance to finish a sentence, but just stood there, grinning, as she shared her reaction to hearing that he wanted to talk to her.

"I always think of you on New Year's Eve," she said. "I always send out a prayer for you and hope you're okay, and that you're happy. I had to wait until tonight to call you and I nearly couldn't stand it."

"It's not night yet," Trevor pointed out.

"I know! Mark said I should just call you already, because I was making him crazy. Do you want to meet? Do you want to come and visit? You could come and stay with us and tell me everything you've been doing..."

"In my whole life?" Trevor asked with a laugh.

"Pretty much," she agreed then laughed herself.

It was right about then that Trevor saw Chynna surrender her wedding ring to Tristan. The bird put it in his stash and Trevor had to look away as the possibility of being with Chynna rose hot in his chest. His desire for that future was almost overwhelming, but he'd learned that she was easily spooked.

He had to take this slow.

And do it right.

His sister proceeded to give him a condensed version of her own life, including her adoptive family, her new name, how she met her husband, and how she'd tried to find him. "You never changed your name at all."

"It's a good name, I think."

"How did I not find you? Aren't you on social media?"

"I just started this week," Trevor admitted with a laugh.

"And an unlisted phone number, I'll bet."

"Cell phones come and go."

She sighed. "It's so wonderful to talk to you."

"Yes, it's really good. I'm sorry I didn't do it sooner."

"Why now?"

"A friend suggested it. Kind of a challenge." He smiled at Chynna who was watching him from the other side of the shop. She smiled back at him and his heart skipped.

"A friend? Are you married?"

"Nope."

"Kids?"

"Nope."

"Well, I have five and trust me that's plenty for both of us." She talked about her kids, their ages and their interests and Trevor just smiled, letting the sound of her happiness roll over him. He remembered now that she'd always been a happy baby, always laughing and gurgling with pleasure. Her voice now sounded a lot like those gurgles. "Jayden said you own restaurants," she said finally, pausing for breath.

"Not any more. I tend to sell them when they're successful and start over."

"Which ones?"

"Well, first in Portland, there was..." Trevor listed his restaurants in order of acquisition, unprepared for his sister to squeal with delight when he named the last one he'd sold in Boston.

"I love that place!" she said.

"It's probably changed. It's been three years since I sold it..."

"But they have the best pavlova for dessert and I just love the view. Oh! You have to meet us there. My daughter—your niece—is getting married there on Valentine's Day. It's going to be beautiful and I know she'd want you to be there. Promise you'll come, and maybe bring your friend."

"I'll have to ask her."

"Look, you must have plans for tonight. Let's trade numbers and talk next week. We can figure out a time, or maybe even a place."

"I'd like that," Trevor agreed, then took a deep breath when he ended the call. He felt shivers running down his spine and shook them off. "Her name's Lindsay now."

"She sounded excited."

Trevor smiled and looked down at his phone. "She was. This call is a much better memory than the one I usually have on this night of the year."

They eyed each other from across the shop, a mountain of emotion between them. Or maybe it was engulfing them. Trevor had never felt so filled with love in his life.

And that meant, he knew what he needed to do.

"You should add a dragon tattoo," Chynna said finally and Trevor was surprised. "A gold one. Maybe a big back piece."

"Why?" As soon as he asked the question Trevor suspected he knew the answer. He remembered the story she'd told him.

"Because you've succeeded. You've persisted and you've made the transformation into who you wanted to be. You jumped the falls and you should get your reward." She smiled.

Trevor reached out and took her hand. "Would you design it for me?"

Her eyes widened in surprise. "Are you sure?"

"Absolutely."

"It'll be a big piece and one you should think about..."

"I always do," he said, interrupting her. "But I also know when something feels right. I'd be honored to have Tristan's design culminate with yours. Will you?"

Chynna swallowed and he saw the tears fill her eyes. "I'd love to." Their gazes clung and she swallowed, speaking in a rush. "A back piece takes time. I won't be able to finish it in just two weeks. It might take us that long to decide on the design."

"I know. I'm okay with having a long-term project together. Are you?"

Chynna nodded.

Trevor looked down at her hand and decided to

go for it. "In fact, I know what I want my reward to be."

"The tattoo? I'll do it for you as a gift, if that's what you want."

Trevor shook his head. "That's really generous, Chynna, but then it would be a kind of a commemorative tattoo, like everything between us was in the past." He dared to meet her gaze and had the sense that she was holding her breath. "I'd like our relationship to continue into the future."

She exhaled. "I don't want you to go to Hawaii," she confessed, her words falling in a rush. "At least, not for good."

"I don't want to go for good either."

"But I don't want to ask you to give up your dream."

"I wouldn't be giving up a single thing." He touched the tarot cards on the counter, just brushing them with his fingertips, before turning to face her. "On the contrary, I'd be starting on a whole new adventure." She smiled and he smiled back, then dropped his voice to a whisper. "Let's make some magic together, Chynna."

Chynna laughed, then took the last step between them. He eased away her tears, knowing they were tears of joy, then bent to kiss her. He knew with all his heart and soul that this was the right choice, that she was the one and that this would be the best adventure of all.

Hawaii was not his future.

Chynna was.

And he knew one way to prove it to her.

They took Tristan back to Chynna's apartment and settled him in. He checked out Trevor's bags, opening the zippers and looking in the pockets. In no time at all, the Jeep keys were in Tristan's hoard.

Chynna was looking for something, but she didn't have to look for long. Tristan's drawing was exactly where she'd thought it was, even though she hadn't looked at it in years. She pulled it out the envelope and laid it on the kitchen table, just looking.

She'd forgotten how good it was.

The drawing depicted a woman, her head bent so her face was obscured. It was Chynna, though, and she knew it because of the other imagery. The woman wore flowing robes, like a Greek goddess, and she was on her knees. In one hand, she held a box with a medusa head on the front of it. Her right hand stretched down into a crevasse of darkness. A man's arm rose out of the shadows, as if he was reaching for help, and the woman had clasped his hand, as if she was pulling him to safety. Easily, despite the obvious differences in their size. She was small and delicate, while he was large and heavily muscled. The crevasse was in the side of an orb large enough to hold the man captive: it looked like a crack in the earth where his arm reached out, and there was a hint of the outline of continents on its surface. It was also a pomegranate though, seeds spilling from one end of the crack. The color was striking, since the man was trapped in burgundy and black, even his skin tinted darker. The woman was the source of light, radiant and hopeful, pulling him from darkness into light. Saving him. Inspiring him. Guiding him.

Chynna shook her head, seeing more in the imagery now than she had all those years before.

Trevor had come to stand beside her, and gave a low whistle after he had studied the drawing. "He really was brilliant, wasn't he?"

Chynna nodded, her fingertips hovering over the lines, a lump in her throat.

"And this would be Persephone?"

She nodded again. "Goddess of darkness and death, abducted by Hades and taken to the underworld to be his queen. But her mother, Demeter, intervened and the gods decided that Persephone had to be returned to the world above because she'd been stolen."

"She'd eaten six pomegranate seeds in her time with Hades," Trevor said. "So, she spent six months of the year in the underworld as queen, which resulted in winter."

Chynna glanced at him.

"Hey, I've read some books." He grinned and she smiled back.

"She owns a box of beauty," Chynna said, indicating the burden in her left hand. "And she can bestow beauty and charisma on others. Her symbol is the medusa, whose gaze can turn those who look upon her to stone."

"And you gave Tristan a medusa."

"Yes," Chynna agreed. "He thought it was a sign. She's said to banish ghosts and assist in communication with the dead."

"Courtesy of her time in the underworld, I'll guess."

"And is said to be able to ensure a painless passing." Chynna hoped she'd helped a bit with that for Tristan. "She's also invoked to find true love."

"Or maybe she just gives secret heart tattoos on the full moon to help people find their own happy ending."

Chynna glanced up, not having thought of it that way.

Trevor gestured to the drawing. "I think he nailed it, actually. This is clearly you. Look at the line of her neck, here, and the way she holds her head. That hand is absolutely like yours. It's incredible work. I can't see her face, but I know it's you."

"I thought he wanted to mark me as his muse."

"Maybe he wanted to celebrate that." Trevor folded his arms across his chest. "Did he struggle with depression? Because this image makes me think that loving you was the light in his darkness."

Chynna was surprised. "But he was the life of the party."

"People with depression often are. They hide their truth, until they can't."

She had to consider that, and remembered half a dozen incidents that hadn't seemed very important at the time but now made sense. "Then it was really wicked of me to leave him."

"No, not if he didn't confide in you. If he didn't trust you enough to tell you the truth, then you can't blame yourself for not seeing it. Be kind to yourself, Chynna. You're kind to everyone else."

"I wish I had realized it."

"You were young," Trevor said and put an arm around her waist. "And you went back. You were there at the end. That's what counts."

She had to wipe away a tear then but something had changed. She no longer felt filled to bursting with regret and sorrow over Tristan's death. She was beginning to see it as his journey, as well as a key element of her own. "Do you think it would be weird to have an image of myself on my back?"

"No, because it's a tribute to who you are and what you bring to the world." He spared her a glance. "Making the world a better place while you're here. I like that. I admire it, and it looks like he did, too." He frowned and studied the drawing. "You could change it a bit and make her less like you, more idealized, but I think it would lose something. Most people won't see the resemblance."

"And there's the question of integrating it with my existing tattoos," she said, speaking almost to herself.

"The box could be open instead of closed," Trevor suggested. "And the roses growing from it."

"That would make them a metaphor for beauty."

Chynna smiled, liking that.

"And not a bad one."

"I have to think about it. And doodle a bit."

"Can we eat first?" He smiled at her.

"You know a place," Chynna guessed and he laughed.

"No, but I want to find all of them. I haven't spent nearly enough time in Manhattan. Did you see that market across the street from Flatiron Five? I want to try all the street food..."

Chynna laughed and let him lead her on. Tristan was perfectly happy now that he was home and already on his perch, tired from his adventure. "We could go dancing at the club," she suggested. "I can probably get us in."

"I don't care what we do," Trevor said as he shrugged into his jacket then pulled her into his embrace. "I want to celebrate. We've banished two shit anniversaries and need to commemorate a new one. We're one hell of a team."

"Pretend there's mistletoe," Chynna whispered, then backed Trevor into the wall and kissed him.

They never did go dancing. They ate and walked and talked. They stopped in at Imagination Ink and Chynna showed Rox's book of dragon tattoos to Trevor for inspiration. They talked about tattoos and Trevor charmed Rox and her partner Niall completely. They ate and walked some more, bought a bottle of champagne and were back at her place by midnight to welcome the new year together. They made love slowly, their gazes clinging, and Chynna felt that she'd finally come home.

When she awakened in the morning, Trevor was gone. He hadn't gone far, because his bag was still there, there was a pot of fresh coffee, and he'd left the Magician card standing against the pot.

Chynna smiled. He was off to make magic.

She took a picture of her back in the mirror and began to doodle, planning the placement of Tristan's design and her commemorative tattoo. Trevor was right: opening the box and giving it a more central position would allow her existing roses to look like they were growing out of it.

She wished she had a picture of his back and where the koi tattoo ended, but she worked from memory, sketching how the waves and lotus blossoms could continue across his back beneath a Chinese dragon. The dragon was gold and coiled with power, poised as if he had just leapt over the falls. She added the waterfall on impulse and was considering the composition when Trevor returned.

She wasn't surprised that he'd brought breakfast or that it smelled delicious. She took a deep breath and knew he'd found the Korean place that made delicious *bao* buns, just around the corner.

"*Lumpia, bahn mi*, street tacos," he said, shaking his head. "This city is going to shake up all my assumptions."

"You love it."

"I do! Because there's got to be a way for a great

chef to incorporate the energy of street food and the fusion of tastes, make it approachable and consistent..." He shook his head. "Sorry. I'm excited about possibilities."

"Me, too," Chynna said, because it was true. His enthusiasm was infectious and his admiration was clear when he checked out her sketch for her back piece. Then Chynna showed him her work for his.

"Wow," he said, his gaze darting over the page. "It's like you read my mind."

Chynna explained where she had questions or options, and they talked about the tattoo, but not about when she'd do it.

"Do you have plans today?" he asked after they'd eaten.

"Not one. Do you?" Chynna asked, guessing it was the right question.

Trevor's eyes lit. "Yes! Will you come with me to check something out?"

"Something?"

"I have a diabolical plan, but will abandon it if you say so."

Chynna laughed. "Of course." She assumed he'd made a reservation for lunch but knew she'd follow him anywhere.

Tristan nodded approval from his perch as they left the apartment hand-in-hand just before noon, and she promised the raven they'd be back soon. He croaked as if in understanding and moved to his perch by the window. He loved to watch the activity in the street below.

Under the Mistletoe

Trevor ran down the stairs ahead of Chynna, then tugged her along the sidewalk toward the subway station. The sun was bright and the air was very cold. Chynna could see their breath when they laughed together. The city was quieter than it had been the night before, though the day seemed filled with promise to Chynna. She felt as if she was embarking on a new adventure, like The Fool, and that made her feel toasty right to her toes.

"Close your eyes," Trevor said when they were at the bottom of the stairs to the station, and she did as instructed, trusting him. "It's a surprise." He led her to the train and ensured that she didn't fall, insisting that she not look at the display. They changed trains once, and she could have guessed where but decided not to. She felt like a kid on Christmas morning.

When they climbed to the street again, she didn't have to open her eyes to know that they were at Penn Station. She would have known its smell anywhere, anytime. Trevor kept her hand in his and she walked beside him, bumping shoulders, feeling the strength of him so close beside her. They crossed the street and went up a block, and she knew they were walking west on 35th. She gripped his hand tightly, a lump in her throat, when she felt the rush of air from the access to the Lincoln Tunnel winding beneath them.

When Trevor stopped, Chynna already knew where they were.

They were at Mythos.

Or where Mythos used to be.

She'd walked to it so many times that there was no doubt in her mind. When she opened her eyes, the building she knew was gone, just as she'd expected. A shining tower filled the block where it had been. It was windy, the way it had always been, the Javits glittering to the west and the river beyond. There were parking lots between the new buildings and she looked beyond the shining new towers. She could point out a dozen places where kids would take refuge each night. Some were already defending their spots and there was a bit of litter blowing.

She blinked away her tears, wanting to share Trevor's excitement but not understanding what it was. "I haven't been here since he died," she said quietly.

"I guessed that." Trevor cleared his throat. "I was checking this out online, because I wanted to see where that part of your life had happened. This morning, I came down here to look."

"It's all different now."

"Not all different," he said, and she knew he'd noticed the kids, too. "Look what I found." He pointed and she didn't understand. She saw then that the new tower had retail spaces on the ground floor. There was a bodega on one corner, with fresh flowers in the window, and a bicycle store beside it. The western corner was a two-story space and it was vacant. That was where Trevor had been pointing. The sign in the window said FOR SALE.

"I don't understand."

"It's the same address as Mythos," he said, stepping toward the black sedan that had just pulled up at the curb. "Come meet the real estate agent. I talked to him this morning on the phone and he agreed to meet us here."

The same address as Mythos.

And they were meeting the agent.

Chynna's heart stopped. Trevor held tightly to her hand as the real estate agent got out of the car and introduced himself. He looked a bit hung over, and they joked about timing. He looked as if he did well in this business, so Chynna guessed he'd meet a potential client anywhere anytime.

He spoke of the amenities that came with the building as he unlocked the door, the square footage, features, demographics of the neighborhood. He barely paused for breath as he led them on a tour of the space. "It's zoned for a restaurant on the street level, though you could probably change that to other retail."

"I'm interested in opening a restaurant," Trevor said and the agent looked relieved.

"It's not always easy to change the zoning, and I think you could do well here." He gestured to the rising towers. "All these hungry people."

Trevor nodded and Chynna knew he'd been thinking the same thing. "What kind of finishing will the developer include?"

Chynna wandered around the space, amazed at the change. She didn't feel a jolt of recognition or the presence of ghosts. She didn't even feel sad. It was a beautiful bright space and even though it was on the same bit of dirt as Mythos, it was all knew.

Like a phoenix rising from the ashes. She smiled, liking that comparison.

The space wasn't just vacant: it still needed to be finished. Floor to ceiling windows filled the two exterior walls, and there were steel beams for the ceiling to go between the two floors.

"They left it open until the location of the stairs is decided," the real estate agent said.

"In the middle," Trevor said without hesitation. "A big sweeping staircase to the second floor. The place needs drama." He glanced at Chynna and she nodded.

"A showpiece," she agreed. "Larger than life." They smiled at each other.

"What about the layout?" the agent asked. "More restaurant seating on the second floor? Kitchen in that corner, so you can get deliveries on the side street?"

Trevor nodded. "And a tattoo shop on the inside corner on the second floor," he said and Chynna felt his gaze upon her. "A boutique space for an artist."

The real estate agent snapped his fingers. "Funny you should suggest that. They said there was a tattoo shop here before…"

"Yes, there was." Chynna said. She crossed the floor and slipped her hand into the warmth of Trevor's.

"Give us a minute?" Trevor asked the agent who

pulled out his phone and made a call as he walked toward his car.

"Same address, different building," Trevor said. "It felt like a sign when I saw the listing."

"Of?"

"A fresh start." He smiled. "A little magic to be made."

"A new adventure," she teased with a smile.

Trevor's gaze searched hers. "I'd like to put down roots, here, where I can be close to my sister and her family, and where I can be close to you, if that's what you want. I intend to turn down the opportunity in Hawaii, and create my own dream, right here."

"I thought the hotel in Hawaii was what you always wanted."

"That was what I thought. You showed me otherwise. You tempted me to reach for more." He turned to face Chynna, his gaze as intent as ever as he held her hands in his, and his next words were husky. "I want to build a restaurant that's here for the duration, one that evolves and yet provides a consistent experience to its customers. I want to try all the street food. I want to pursue loyalty instead of trends, and I never want to sell out." He looked down at her hands and she watched him swallow. "I want to take your challenge. I want to build on the legacy of what Tristan taught you and make this world a better place, because I was here. There are still kids here, still kids who need a chance. I'd like to be here, to be part of this community, and give kids that chance."

Chynna's heart clenched because it was such a perfect idea.

But Trevor wasn't done. "I'd like to call the restaurant Tristan's in his memory. As a tribute."

"That would be wonderful," Chynna whispered, knowing that she could honor his memory now without being haunted by his loss. "But I think we should call it Phoenix instead."

"Phoenix. I like that."

"Otherwise, people will think we named it after my pet raven."

Trevor laughed. "Good point! I'd like to have a soup kitchen once a week, the day we're closed, and maybe host cooking classes for the people who live nearby. I want this place to become a neighborhood fixture. We could sponsor a farmers' market nearby."

"Or a food truck festival."

"Yes!" He took a breath. "I don't know a lot about building permanence, Chynna, but I really want to learn. You showed me how important it was to reach out to Joanna and I have a family now."

"You'll do fine," Chynna said, thinking he needed reassurance.

"I hope so, but I want more. You've got me started and now I want it all."

"You don't do half-measures."

He grinned and shook his head. "All in or all out." He leaned down to touch his nose to hers. "Any chance you'll go all in with me? There's only one artist I'd like to have in that tattoo shop upstairs, only one fit to carry on the legacy."

Chynna smiled. "So, you'd like a business partner?"

"More than that, Chynna. So much more than that. There's a two bedroom apartment for sale immediately above this, if you wanted to live here, with me, and build a future. You, me and a raven who reads tarot cards." Trevor swallowed and his words faltered. He dropped to one knee, still holding her hands, his movement creating a little cloud of sawdust, and she finally realized what he was going to say. "I love you, Chynna. Will you marry me and be my partner in every way?"

"Yes!" She held up a finger. "But on one condition."

Trevor looked surprised for a moment.

"I want to go to Hawaii with you. Not to stay. Just to check it out. They do a lot of great tattoo work there, and you could might get some inspiration or advice from your friend there."

His smile was filled with relief. "You have the best ideas," he murmured. "We are the best team." Chynna had no chance to agree because he drew her into his arms for a celebratory kiss.

She kissed him back, knowing that she'd found what she didn't even realize she needed, and their future together would be bright indeed.

She was going to blame it on that mistletoe, the magic of the original secret heart tattoo, and a Christmas wedding in Honey Hill.

Deborah Cooke

୪

*Secret Heart Ink is a spin-off series
from Deborah's contemporary romance series,*
Flatiron Five.

SIMPLY IRRESISTIBLE

ADDICTED TO LOVE

IN THE MIDNIGHT HOUR

SOME GUYS HAVE ALL THE LUCK

GOING TO THE CHAPEL

BAD CASE OF LOVING YOU

SOME LIKE IT HOT
Coming in 2020

☙

ABOUT THE AUTHOR

Deborah Cooke sold her first book in 1992, a medieval romance called **Romance of the Rose** published under her pseudonym Claire Delacroix. Since then, she has published over fifty novels in a wide variety of sub-genres, including historical romance, contemporary romance, and paranormal romance. She has published under the names Claire Delacroix, Claire Cross and Deborah Cooke. **The Beauty**, part of her successful Bride Quest series of historical romances, was her first title to land on the *New York Times* List of Bestselling Books. Her books routinely appear on other bestseller lists and have won numerous awards. In 2009, she was the writer-in-residence at the Toronto Public Library, the first time the library has hosted a residency focused on the romance genre. In 2012, she was honored to receive the Romance Writers of America's Mentor of the Year Award.

Currently, she writes paranormal romances and contemporary romances as Deborah Cooke. She also writes historical romances as Claire Delacroix. Deborah lives in Canada with her husband and family, as well as far too many unfinished knitting projects.

To learn more about her books, visit her websites:
http://deborahcooke.com
http://delacroix.net

Under the Mistletoe

CPSIA information can be obtained
at www.ICGtesting.com
Printed in the USA
FSHW010124120120
65892FS

9 781989 367452